All Darling Children

KATRINA MONROE

Unlocking New Worlds

Print ISBN-13: 978-1-940215-78-5
Print ISBN-10: 1-940215-78-1

Red Adept Publishing, LLC
104 Bugenfield Court
Garner, NC 27529
http://RedAdeptPublishing.com/

Cover and Formatting: Streetlight Graphics

To the lost boys and girls who haven't yet found Neverland.
Keep looking.

The boys on the island vary, of course, in numbers, according as they get killed and so-on; and when they seem to be growing up, which is against the rules, Peter thins them out.

Peter Pan by J.M. Barrie

Chapter One

MADGE JUMPED FROM HER SECOND-STORY bedroom window, landing sideways on a pile of leaves. Her shoulder jammed, her fist flew up, and she clocked herself in the jaw. Pain rocketed through her arm and throbbed on the sides of her face, but she couldn't stop moving, not even for a second. She rolled from the pile—damp leaves clung to her hair and legs—and ran. Her pack banged against her back, heavy with supplies: a half-empty peanut butter jar, a serrated kitchen knife, granola bars, and a liter bottle of water. Tucked into the side pocket was a bundle of cash—about a hundred and fifty dollars—that she'd saved from raking the neighbors' lawns. She'd even taken the bags away herself—*it's no problem, really*—and dumped them outside her window just after dark.

Weeks of planning had gone into tonight's escape. She would *not* fuck it up.

Streetlights flickered overhead, casting distorted shadows over the street. It smelled every bit like autumn outside—all cool air, burning wood, and Starbucks cups sticky with pumpkin spice. It was colder than Madge thought it would be, and she wished she'd packed a thicker jacket. She shrugged off the thought. *Too late now.* She figured she could buy (or steal) one when she got to Chicago.

When she'd first decided to go to the Windy City, it seemed like an impossible task. She was broke, carless, and not to mention, fourteen years old. To any adult, the four-hundred-mile trip from Anoka, Minnesota, to Chicago was a weekend road trip, easily completed in an afternoon. To Madge, Chicago might as well have been on the other side of the world. But once it became clear she had no other choice, she found a way.

Bus tickets were criminally easy to get, provided one had a phone and a credit card. The difficult part had been keeping her plans from Grandma Wendy. Madge had stolen Grandma Wendy's credit card for the tickets and stalked the mailbox for any incoming statements that could rat her out. She'd used the same card tonight to call for a taxi, which would pick her up from the drugstore and bring her to the bus station.

Madge kept to the side streets, cutting through alleys between apartment buildings. The drugstore wasn't far, but she couldn't be too careful. Grandma Wendy had eyes and ears all over the neighborhood. If she could have gotten away with microchipping Madge like a dog, she probably would have. Madge slowed to a walk, pulling her sweater's hood down low over her face.

Gap-toothed pumpkins grinned at her from windows and stoops. Cardboard headstones decorated lawns with lame epitaphs like "Ima Goner" and "RIP Green Bay Packers." She heard the high-pitched voice of Mrs. Jensen, the Historical Society president and resident blowhard, detailing the supposed ghost sightings along Main Street to a group of tourists. Madge cut left through someone's backyard, avoiding the route of the ghost tour. Unlike most of her town—self-proclaimed Halloween capital of the world—Madge didn't like Halloween. She'd had enough of masks and secrets to last a lifetime.

She spotted the glow of the drugstore across the street and breathed deeply, trying to slow her hammering heart. A few more minutes and she'd be on her way to Chicago, away from Grandma Wendy forever. She jogged across the street and paced the sidewalk. She checked her watch. Ten fifty-seven. A little more than fifteen minutes to go.

The air chilled quickly, the temperature dropping with every minute. Her breath puffed little white clouds. She wondered how cold it'd be in Chicago and if she'd even be there long enough to find out. Would she be welcomed with open arms or shipped back to Grandma Wendy's talons? Anxiety bubbled in Madge's gut. She was running out of chances. With each new plan, Grandma Wendy wised up, always one step ahead.

Twenty minutes passed. Thirty.

Her nose and ears felt numb. She tried to wait inside, but the pimple-faced clerk kicked her out, probably thinking she was a shoplifter. Madge was on the edge of giving up when headlights turned the corner and slowed. The corners of her mouth lifted. She went to wave. Blue-and-red lights punctured the dark.

Shit.

She ran. The roar of the cop car's engine was like a lion, hot on her trail with the scent of her blood in its nose. Tears pricked the corners of her eyes as a freezing gust smacked her face. Her vision blurred, and her toe caught a dip in the sidewalk. She hit the concrete with an audible smack, and her face slid across it like sandpaper. Pain churned her stomach, but she was on her feet and moving before she could even see straight. A car door slammed, and the cop yelled. His footfalls seemed to shake the sidewalk. Curious faces peered out their windows as she passed and wanted to scream for help, but she knew how it looked: a delinquent kid running from her crimes. It never occurred to them that maybe *she* was the victim. *She* was the one who needed saving.

Madge turned the corner, calves and lungs burning, but the cop was too fast. She reached a fence, ready to climb, but the cop's hands were on her, pulling her to the ground.

"Jesus, kid," the cop muttered between pants. "Why do you always have to run?"

Her face was in the dirt, and she had to twist her neck hard to the right to breathe. "Why do you always have to chase me, Officer Douche Bag?"

He grunted. "You're lucky your grandma's a friend. Any other kid and I'd have your ass in juvie tonight."

"Yeah. Lucky."

He slapped handcuffs on her wrists—probably payback for the douche-bag comment—and yanked her to her feet by her elbows. She spat out a chunk of grass.

"Your grandma's worried sick, you know," Officer DB said. "All you kids, so ungrateful."

Madge fell silent. She'd heard this before. How lucky she was to have someone like Grandma Wendy in her life to pick up where Madge's mother had left off. The story, as Grandma Wendy liked to tell it, was that Madge's mother, overwhelmed by the demands of a hellish four-year-old Madge, ditched her at Grandma Wendy's place only to run off and die in an accident.

Lies. All of it.

Officer DB took the entire walk back to his car to catch his breath. Madge stood next to the passenger door, expecting to ride up front like every other time. Instead, with a dickish grin on his face, he opened the back door.

"You're kidding."

"You think you're big enough to run off to God knows where, you're big enough to ride in the back." He put a sausage-fingered hand on her head and stuffed her in the car. "Try not to touch anything. Haven't had the chance to clean it."

Madge shuddered, gagging on the stench of something sour and rotten.

Officer DB drove with the roof lights on, giving rubberneckers a good look at the girl in the back. He was trying to shame her into not running off again, but Madge was already planning her next move.

Soon, the yard came into view, illuminated by a pair of antique lanterns that'd seen more care and attention from Grandma Wendy than Madge had seen in her lifetime. The yard itself was all sharp angles—squared lawn and driveway, a brick-lined path, and empty flower boxes. All of the lights in Grandma Wendy's house were on. The door flew open, and she stood in the mint-green doorway like Hansel and Gretel's witch. Arms crossed, Grandma Wendy made no show of meeting Madge at the car. They'd done this too many times.

Office DB made Madge climb out without the use of her hands, and she biffed it on the roof more than once. She could almost feel the smirks. Officer DB and the witch were enjoying this. Madge's face grew hot, and her hands balled into fists. She'd been so careful. *How did Grandma Wendy always know?*

Cuffs off, Officer DB escorted Madge to the door. She breezed past Grandma Wendy without a word, marching up to her room where she knew she'd find the place torn apart, her computer confiscated, and the window resealed. Back to square one. The front door slammed.

Grandma Wendy's voice carried up the stairwell. "I can't believe you, Margaret. Of all days..."

Madge bit her lip hard enough to bleed. She wouldn't be baited.

"It's like you don't even care."

Madge bristled. *She* was one to talk. The rest of the year, Grandma ignored Madge the minute her mother came into the conversation. Her mother might as well have not existed. But tomorrow was the tenth anniversary of Madge's mother's supposed death. There would be a memorial service and special brunch in her mother's honor.

But what Grandma Wendy refused to admit—what Madge had been holding in the smallest corner of her heart like the most precious treasure—was that Madge's mother was alive.

Chapter Two

SHE COULDN'T PINPOINT THE MOMENT she'd first realized it, but on some level, like the lizard part of a person's brain that twitched at an invisible threat, Madge always knew. The inconsistency in the little details of Grandma Wendy's stories, the absence of any witnesses, friends, or anyone who knew Madge's mother before… It was all wrong, and Madge knew it.

With the help of the Internet, Madge located a woman living in Chicago who was the closest match to the woman Madge remembered her mother to be. The profile picture on the woman's Facebook page was dark, but familiar. The woman—Jane—regularly posted articles on what it meant to be a mother, though Madge could never find any evidence of children. It was like she was calling out to Madge. *Come find me. I miss you.*

I miss you too, Madge thought as she stared at her bedroom door the next morning. After her first escape, Grandma Wendy had Uncle Michael switch the knob so that it locked from the outside. Madge had learned to hold her bladder until the old crone decided to let her out. Caged, like an animal, she wondered what her mother would think if she knew.

At exactly eight a.m., the lock clicked.

"Dressed and downstairs in thirty minutes," Grandma Wendy said through the door.

Madge flipped her middle finger so hard it hurt.

She waited until Grandma Wendy's footsteps disappeared downstairs before opening the door. Hanging on the knob was a black dress with puffy sleeves and a lace collar that looked like a bib.

As though reading her mind, Grandma Wendy called, "Put on the dress, Margaret."

Madge sneered—at both the dress and the use of her given name—and snatched the thing from the hanger. Unfortunately, it didn't rip.

After spending fifteen minutes trying to tame her black curls, she twisted the mess into a ponytail, which fell almost to the center of her back. People said Madge looked like her mother. They were lying. Madge had seen pictures. Her favorite was one in which her mother was maybe sixteen, mouth open wide in the kind of laugh that made your stomach hurt for hours afterward. Her brown eyes squinted, and her body contorted like she was being electrocuted. It was... goofy, and it was how Madge liked to think of her, as someone who would smile at Madge, not sneer the way Grandma Wendy did.

Madge descended into the living room to find Grandma Wendy in her favorite chair, curled over a book. The lace neck of her dress strained against her old-person neck skin. Madge had seen the book before and had even looked inside it once. She'd read the first four words before Grandma Wendy snatched it out of her hands and grounded her. It read like a diary, but the way Grandma Wendy teared up over it and the fact that she only pulled it from the shelf on the anniversary of her daughter's death made Madge believe it was something more.

Uncle Michael stood in the corner with a tumbler of amber liquid in his hands, his unblinking eyes fixed on his sister.

"This dress is ridiculous," Madge said.

Uncle Michael snapped out of his trance, but Grandma Wendy only seemed to fall deeper into her own thoughts. "You look lovely," he said.

Madge snorted. The dress was at least a size too small, hugging her ass and hips in a way that—if not for the gap where her breasts ought to be—was almost porny.

A long, awkward moment passed. Grandma Wendy finally stuffed her book—the spine emblazoned with golden initials, W.D. for Wendy Darling—back on the shelf. She took one long look at Madge and nodded. "You don't quite fill it out the way I'd like, but..."

Madge scowled. It was bad enough she caught hell from the girls in the locker room at school for her lack of *development*. Flatsy Patsy, they called her.

"Nothing we can do about that," Grandma Wendy finished. "Did you try on that padded brassiere I bought you?"

The way she said *brassiere* with more syllables than necessary—the fact that she even said *brassiere*—was a remnant of Grandma's youth in England. She didn't talk about it. The Darlings may have been a family built on strength of character, but they survived because of their secrets.

"Yes," Madge lied. She'd burned the thing in effigy atop a pile of leaves. "Doesn't fit."

Grandma Wendy raised an eyebrow. Accusation flickered in her eyes. A terrifying second passed in which Madge figured she'd been caught in one of a thousand lies she'd told over the last few months. *Ladies don't lie*—one of a hundred platitudes drilled into Madge's mind where "I love you" and "be careful" should have been. It was dangerous to think what else Grandma Wendy could do to her because Madge didn't want to know the answer.

"We should get going." Uncle Michael's words slurred a bit. "We'll be late."

St. Andrew's Catholic Church towered over the surrounding cityscape, its spires like long-nailed fingers reaching for the sky. The front archway seemed to swallow the door, and every time Madge stepped through it, no matter how much taller she'd grown, she shrank to the size of a thimble as she crossed the threshold. The two dark windows over the arch became eyes, and the door, a great mouth.

Inside, however, was another world. If not for the sea of black, Madge thought they wouldn't know they were there for a memorial service. The ceiling was high, illuminated by the sun's rays refracting through stained-glass windows of the saints and the Virgin. The colors flicked over the twenty or so faces that had come to pay respects to Madge's mother. Her portrait stood on an easel, framed in violets. Madge hated it. Her mother's lips were set in a disapproving line, and her hair was piled on top of her head, put away like a nuisance. She looked *sad*. It was only when Madge saw this portrait that she felt something like grief.

Grandma Wendy wrapped her arm around Madge's shoulder and forcibly guided her to the front row. Madge caught the sympathetic glances from people whose names she'd never remember and turned her attention to prying the grit from beneath her nails with the long end of the gold cross that hung around her neck. *Poor motherless Margaret.* For the next few hours, she expected to be poked and groped by the dry, rice-paper hands of Grandma's friends and extended family. Aunt Liza liked to kiss her, which wouldn't be so bad if her breath didn't smell like rancid beets.

The front pew was reserved for the immediate family. There were only three of them, leaving the rest of the pew cold and empty. Madge sat between Uncle Michael and Grandma Wendy, slouching as low as she could without sliding to the floor.

"It'll be over soon, kid." Uncle Michael patted her shoulder. Out of the corner of her eye, she saw the nubby remains of two fingers. When Madge was eight, she'd resolved to ask him what happened—out of Grandma's earshot. The opportunity still hadn't presented itself.

"Quiet, Michael," Grandma Wendy snapped.

The priest stepped up to the pulpit, and the murmur of the crowd waned. He nodded in the direction of their pew before beginning. "Good morning, brothers and sisters. Today, we come together to celebrate the life and mourn the tragic passing of Jane Darling."

Madge gripped the edge of the pew and bit her tongue. She wanted to shout, "Mom's alive!", to knock the ugly portrait from its easel, set fire to the whole assembly, and run screaming from the chaos until she was in Chicago, reunited with her mother.

The priest continued, "On this sad day, we have no answers to the question, 'Why could Jane not be left to her family for longer?' We cannot explain, but we do what we can: offer the family our sympathy and support at this time." He glanced at Grandma Wendy. "We also assure you of our prayers. I would also like to assure you of something else: that Jane's death is not Jesus's fault, that God is not to blame for it."

Throughout the reading, Madge studied Grandma Wendy's face for signs of emotion. When the priest glanced in Grandma's Wendy's direction, her face softened, and the corners of her eyes drooped. When he looked away, any lingering wrinkle of grief smoothed. Whatever hostility Grandma Wendy felt for Madge, she felt for Madge's mother too. It should have upset Madge. What kind of woman hated her own kid? But instead, Madge found comfort in the idea that she and her mother at least shared one thing and that they were supposed to be together.

Uncle Michael muttered something like, "No, *he's* to blame." Grandma shot him an icy glare.

Madge perked up.

He? He, who? Her father? Madge knew less about him than she did about her mother. Once, when Uncle Michael had found the bottom of a whiskey bottle—he tended to find a lot of whiskey-bottle bottoms— he let slip that he knew Madge's father. Grandma Wendy had claimed no one knew who he was, that Madge was an *unwanted bastard*. Grandma Wendy's words.

The priest droned on about faith and forgiveness and other feel-good words that meant less than nothing. Madge tuned out. She needed another escape plan and fast. With the memorial fresh in her mind, Grandma Wendy would be distracted. If there was ever going to be another chance to actually reach Chicago, tonight was it.

At the end of the sermon, Madge stood next to the portrait, struggling not to fidget with the dress. It dug into the soft flesh beneath her breasts, and every time she breathed in, she worried she'd puncture a lung.

Aunt Liza—not really an aunt, but the kind of woman who insisted on being considered a relative—was first in line to place a daisy beneath the easel. She leaned in to kiss Madge, who instinctively held her breath. It didn't help. Instead of beets on Aunt Liza's breath, it was onions and cigarette smoke. Aunt Liza held Madge's face to plant a wet lip print on her forehead. For a moment, she looked at Madge as though wanting to tell her something. When Madge was younger, she'd gravitated toward Aunt Liza when it became clear Grandma Wendy had no interest in Madge's feelings. Beet breath and all, she'd been a kind of safe place until Grandma Wendy had words with her. After that, Madge wasn't allowed to play at Aunt Liza's anymore. She hadn't known it as a betrayal at the time. She only knew she was alone and angry, and the people she'd wanted to turn to wouldn't—or couldn't—listen. Madge forced a smile—all teeth—to make the woman go away.

By the time the last of the mourners dropped a flower for her mother, Madge's face was sticky with spit and lipstick. She wanted to get home to change and wash her face and pack, but there was still brunch to deal with.

People fidgeted in their seats, seemingly as anxious as Madge was to get out of the church. Despite the cold outside, the place was stuffy, and the underlying stench of B.O. permeated.

The priest quieted them with raised arms. "If there is no one else who wishes to give their condolences to the Darling family…"

Splitting the silence like a crack of thunder, a rooster's crow filled the church. It vibrated beneath Madge's feet and knocked the portrait of her mother off the easel. Grit and rotten wood from somewhere in the rafters trickled down on the crowd. Someone shouted, "Earthquake!" The priest cowered behind the altar, and guests ran for the door.

"Wendy!" Uncle Michael said.

Madge turned and spotted Grandma Wendy sprawled over the steps leading to the pulpit, hands clutching her chest.

Michael fell to his knees and shook Grandma Wendy's shoulders. His face paled. "She's not breathing."

From the Diary of Wendy Moira Angela Darling

It was like magic.

I've told the story a hundred times (it's John's favorite) and never once has he actually appeared at the window until last night. Just as I reached the bit about Captain Hook being chased through the forests of Neverland by the Lost Boys, I heard giggling outside the window. I went to check and, at first, saw nothing but the new-fallen snow on the sidewalk below. Streetlamps illuminated the entire block. Still, I saw nothing.

Just the wind, I thought. I should have looked up.

"And then the Lost Boys caught the pirates!" Michael shouted.

I shushed him. Mother and Father were asleep in the next room. "Yes. Of course they did."

"And then what?" John asked.

I took a chance and ever so slightly turned my face toward the window. He smiled from behind the frosted glass. His teeth were like baby pearls, and his face... Never had I seen a boy so handsome. His hair collected snowflakes as he hovered outside the window. He gestured for me to continue.

With a real audience, I told the story with more color. The pirates weren't mean and angry. They were vicious and frightening. I used my entire body—flashing a view of my new nightgown in its full length toward the window more than once—to relay the tale. When I'd finished, I was simply exhausted.

"That was the best story ever," John said.

With butterflies in my gut, I raced to the window and threw it open. A blast of cool air and swirling snow engulfed the room. I needed to know what he thought. Had I gotten it right? What had I missed? But Peter Pan was already gone.

Chapter Three

THE DOCTOR WASN'T HANDSOME, BUT when he smiled, it was easy to imagine that he once was. Madge never had much luck with boys. They were irritating at best and testosterone-fueled wastes of skin at worst. Her friend Jennifer suggested Madge try being a lesbian. She couldn't get into that either. The doctor bought Madge an orange soda from the machine in the waiting room and told her that Grandma Wendy'd had a heart attack. "Do you know what that means?"

"Is she dead?"

It came off harder than she meant, but she didn't correct herself.

The doctor blinked. "No. We removed the clot, so she's going to be fine."

Madge sipped the soda. It was too sweet, but the bubbles settled her stomach. Part of her was relieved. Kind of. The other part…

"We're going to keep her overnight, maybe two, just to keep an eye on her. Do you have someone you can stay with?"

Her mind blanked. She'd never stayed anywhere other than Grandma Wendy's house, with only the old woman for company. No sleepovers. No visitors after dark. But none of that was important now. They were keeping her overnight. An entire night without the vulture-like gaze on Madge's every move. It was fate.

"I can stay with my Uncle Michael. He's the one who checked her in."

Once a nurse managed to find him—curled over a cup of lukewarm coffee—Uncle Michael didn't object to the arrangement. In fact, he seemed relieved to not have to be alone.

"I've got a fold-out couch," he said. "Not much, but it'll do for now."

"I'd rather sleep in my bed," she said, a little too quickly. "I'd feel safer there."

Uncle Michael nodded. "Of course."

Madge almost felt bad about the wrath he'd catch once Grandma Wendy realized Madge was gone for good. Almost, but not quite.

Madge and Uncle Michael visited Grandma Wendy in her room, but the medications didn't allow her to stay conscious for long. During intermittent periods of wakefulness, she stared dreamily at the ceiling, fluttering her fingers over the hospital-issue blanket as if she were playing her piano. She looked frail—properly old—and not at all intimidating, as if her protective shell fell away, revealing this slight, strange woman wearing Grandma Wendy's face. Madge tapped her cold, powdery hand, careful not to touch the IV protruding from a purple vein, expecting her to take a swipe at Madge's face. It wouldn't have been the first time. A faint pink scar bisected her earlobe where Grandma Wendy had swung open-handed, and her wedding ring snagged Madge's earring, tearing it clear through the flesh. Now that she thought about it, Madge couldn't remember the reason for the fight. All she remembered was the look of anger and surprise on Grandma Wendy's face. She'd sent Madge to her room and didn't speak to her for days.

Now, though, Grandma Wendy wouldn't be touching anyone. Madge's heart fluttered with a mix of dread and anticipation. The doctor who'd bought her the soda walked in, carrying a chart. He winked at Madge then led Uncle Michael to the corner where they did that annoying adult thing where they insulted Madge's intelligence by whispering. She eavesdropped, one hand expertly navigating the bureau for Grandma Wendy's wallet.

"Normally, in these situations we want to be aware of next of kin, just in case," the doctor said.

Uncle Michael sighed, and it seemed to take a lot out of him. "That's me. I'm her brother."

"And who is Peter? Husband?"

Michael's face paled. "Excuse me?"

Madge stuffed the wallet into her bag. She wondered where Grandma Wendy hid her computer and who the hell Peter was.

The doctor flipped through the chart. "When Mrs. Darling was first coming out of the anesthesia, she yelled the name. Scared the shi—" He glanced at Madge. "The bejeezus out of the nurse."

Uncle Michael shrugged, but his back and arms were stiff. "Probably just a dream."

The doctor seemed unsure, but he dropped the subject and moved on to the technical aspects of her attack. Boring. Madge stopped listening and watched the monitor *bleep, bleep, bleep* the unsteady rhythm of Grandma Wendy's heartbeat.

In fourth grade, Madge's teacher had assigned the class an ancestry project. She gave them each a poster-board tree and told them to fill in the branches with names and birthdays of the members of their families as far back as they could go. Grandma Wendy refused to help, so Madge could only fill in six names, all of them Darlings. *Ask me today how many I can name, and I'll give you the same answer*, Madge thought.

With Grandma Wendy in the hospital, though, Madge was left with one. Uncle Michael escorted her from the hospital, stopping first at the gift shop to buy her a package of gummy bears that she didn't ask for. Old men with no children, if television was to be believed, comforted with food rather than words. His car was a wood-paneled station wagon with rusted wheel wells. Inside, the vinyl seats were torn, and bits of duct tape snagged her dress. The air vent kicked on and burped out a smell like smoke and piss.

Uncle Michael stared straight out the windshield as he drove, barely breathing. He'd been drinking—Madge had seen him snatch a few gulps from the flask in his jacket—and was trying to appear sober for her benefit. She wanted to tell him that she wasn't Grandma Wendy, that she liked that he was at least kind of normal. Normal people drank when they were in over their head. Normal people didn't force their grandchildren into solitude and then refuse to voice any valid reason for the isolation. If it wasn't for a visit from the truant officer the same year as the family-tree project—a result of too many absences—Grandma Wendy would probably have tried to keep her away from school altogether. Not that it made much difference. Madge was alone there too. Even the teachers thought her family was cursed.

There were rumors. Grandma Wendy was crazy and had murdered her brother and daughter. Madge's mother was a gypsy. Uncle Michael was in cahoots with the devil—those sorts of things. She took none of them seriously, though she thought she might have liked being raised by a gypsy. What Madge wouldn't give to curse some of her classmates with diarrhea of the mouth, since they seemed to enjoy gossip so much.

The house was dark, but Madge had spent the better part of her life navigating its halls, looking for ways to sneak out without setting off the security alarm. She had no problem finding the stairs.

Uncle Michael walked face-first into the hat stand. "Fucking bloody awful way to organize your house."

Madge flipped a switch that flooded the entire front of the house with light. Grandma Wendy was a collector, not of one type of object, but of anything that, she said, made her *feel*. Madge had a hard time believing the woman felt anything other than anger. The foyer walls were covered in framed photographs from various antique shops. They weren't famous people or relatives, and they were all young men. Uncle Michael called them her lost boys, but only when she wasn't around. Furniture took up most of the space in the living room—none of the pieces matched—and was otherwise empty of decoration. Her bookshelf dominated the far wall.

"Oh." Michael glanced down the hall toward the kitchen. "Thanks."

Madge started up the stairs and announced over her shoulder, "I'm going to bed."

"It's only seven."

Madge shrugged. "School tomorrow."

He nodded, probably drawing on his inexperience and what he thought Grandma Wendy would deem appropriate for a young lady. He started to follow her up the stairs.

"What are you...?"

"Just... checking."

Uncle Michael passed her on the stairs and headed straight for her room—easy to find since it was the only open door on the floor. Grandma

Wendy had a thing about drafts. Most of the windows were caulked shut. Madge's were newly barred. Grandma Wendy must've planned it as a post-memorial surprise—or warning. *Bitch.* Uncle Michael slid the window open and tested their strength. He grunted and nodded.

"Well." He stepped toward Madge, arms open in an awkward attempt at affection, which she ignored. He managed a half-smile. "Sleep well, kid."

"Thanks."

"She'll be okay, ya know."

"Yep."

After he left the room—keeping the door open a crack—she changed into flannel pants and a hoodie and lay in bed on top of the covers. He was still Grandma Wendy's brother; suspicion ran in their blood. He'd sit up, listening for her movements for a while, and then dig into the liquor cabinet.

For the next hour, Madge pretended to sleep.

Chapter Four

NCLE MICHAEL WASN'T A LARGE man, but a lifetime of binge drinking had built up a tolerance to the poison. It was nearly midnight by the time his slow, scraping footsteps between the kitchen and the living room stopped. Too late to shop for a bus ticket, but she wasn't about to waste this chance. Madge waited another ten minutes, and then, with steps so light she might as well have been flying, she made her way out into the hallway.

Peering downstairs was pointless. She only saw the flicker of the television, and the sound was low. She remembered from her previous adventures that the fifth and ninth stairs creaked, so she counted silently and straddled over them as she descended. Madge forgot, however, the loose floorboard at the end of staircase and nearly face-planted on the hardwood, catching herself on the bannister. She righted herself and listened. Hearing nothing but the television, she continued into the foyer for a better look at the kitchen.

It was a disaster: ice trays strewn over the counter, empty wine bottles lined up like bowling pins with one tipped on its side, the contents a bloody red mess on the tile. The cabinets hung open, presumably from Michael's search for Grandma Wendy's stash, which was limited to "special occasion" wines and the rare bottle of scotch, reserved for after the memorial to toast her daughter's memory.

She passed through the kitchen and on to the living room, where Uncle Michael snored in Grandma Wendy's chair. Tucked between his legs was the scotch bottle, half empty. Phlegm gargled at the back of his throat with each inhale, and she made a note to turn his head before leaving the room so he didn't choke on his own vomit.

She still had the knife, peanut butter, and granola in her backpack from last night. She stuffed Grandma Wendy's wallet in the bottom along with an extra jacket and, on a whim, snatched Grandma Wendy's mystery book from the shelf. She'd need something to read on the bus, and if the book was what Madge thought it was, it'd make for an interesting ride.

Uncle Michael coughed, and his eyes flew open for an instant. Madge held her breath, barely hidden by the back of another chair. His eyes rolled back, and he passed out again, this time, with his head turned.

With one last look around the room—did she need anything else?— she slipped on her sneakers. Part of her couldn't believe she was finally going to get away with it. She smiled, thinking of all the things she was going to say to her mother once she found her. How grateful her mother would be. How proud.

Outside, a breeze rushed through the trees. Leaves fell in waves, settling in heaps in the grass. Madge could barely see the street under the piss-yellow streetlights. The sidewalk was a shadow, and the houses on either side of the street were tombs. A lingering fear of the dark whispered in her ear. *Turn back. Wait until dawn.* But in her guts she knew it'd be too late. Now or never.

She forced herself not to run. A jogger drew her attention. *Just out for a midnight stroll, Officer, thanks. Clearing my head.* She figured she'd walk to the bus depot—about seven miles, not too far—and buy a ticket for Chicago the second they opened. To keep her mind off the beasties lurking behind every fence and beneath every porch step, Madge hummed the melody to a song she couldn't name. It was one she'd always known.

She stuck to the main road. Occasional cars rushing past provided a kind of comfort against the deepening darkness. She left the Anoka city limits, and traffic lights grew further apart. Fewer cars appeared down this far, and streetlights flickered from neglect. Madge wrapped her arms around her middle, trying to make herself smaller and less attractive to wandering vagrants looking for some cash or a girl to help them pass the time between meth hits. It wasn't until she hit a stretch of road without a sidewalk and practically no light to see by that she thought this might have been a bad idea.

Nocturnal creatures rustled in the brush, jackhammering her pulse to dangerous levels. A branch cracked. Madge jumped back, and someone behind her laughed. She spun around, holding her breath. The sidewalk was empty.

"Hearing things," she muttered.

She quickened her pace. There was a gas station a few blocks up. She figured she'd see if they had a flashlight. Or pepper spray.

A whistle came from above. She didn't look. Instead, she ran. Though the only sound was her own footsteps, she couldn't shake the feeling of something gaining on her. A breath. A presence. If she stopped, it'd slam right into her. A shadow. A ghost. A whimper caught in her throat. God, she was an idiot. Tomorrow, they'd find her crumpled body on the side of the road.

Something grazed the top of her head, and she screamed. A shadow passed overhead and landed in front of her, blocking her path.

Her muscles tingled, and her brain fought her fear for control.

Run. Don't run. Can't run.

The shadow laughed.

"What do you want?" Madge's voice came out in barely more than a whisper.

A car flew past, but Madge was too scared to wave it down. The headlights strobed across the shadow, and she realized it wasn't a shadow at all. He was a boy. He couldn't be older than Madge, with black hair that looked like it'd been cut with a sharp rock and green eyes so pale they were almost white. He wore a brown poncho, belted at the waist. The frayed edges of it were stained with something dark.

Not a ghost. A boy. Probably a nutjob, judging by the clothes. Knees still a little shaky, she stepped around him. "Halloween's next week, freak. Ditch the outfit, and maybe make it through the night without getting jumped."

He smiled. "Impossible. No one gets the jump on me."

"'Kay."

She gripped the straps of her bag. Crazy people could still rob you.

27

She glanced over her shoulder. The boy was gone. She turned back to the sidewalk only to stop dead. Like magic, he was in front of her again.

"How did you do that?"

"Pixie dust."

What a whack-a-doo. Probably wandered off from some facility. She drifted around him again, keeping a longer distance. This time, he followed.

"Don't follow me."

His smile was condescending and eerily similar to Grandma Wendy's. "I've been following since you left the house. You have a lovely singing voice."

A chill shot through her body. A fucking stalker. Great. If Grandma Wendy wasn't such a freak about technology, Madge would have a cell phone she could use to call for help. But no. She was going to die out of *principle*.

"Look, I don't know what you want, but you need to back off, okay?"

He was on her heels now. "I want *you*, Margaret Darling."

Madge swung her fist wide, hitting only air. His laughter seemed to come from every direction at once. She took off at a sprint. If she could just make it to the gas station...

"Why are you running, silly girl?"

She looked up. The boy flew above her head. Unable to tear her eyes from him, she didn't see a branch in the sidewalk. Her foot caught it, and she started to fall forward, but the boy grabbed her by the backpack. He lifted her an inch off the ground—her stomach flipped—and set her down in front of the branch.

Madge hunched forward, out of breath. Her mind fogged. She must have been dreaming.

The boy crossed his arms and squinted. "You don't know who I am?"

"Seriously?"

He paced like an agitated cat. "I didn't think she'd actually go through with it, not a second time. Oh, Wendy, Wendy, Wendy."

Another car passed, and in the headlight beam, something attached to his belt glinted. He looked up and noticed Madge staring at the dagger. "Oh, don't worry. I'm not going to hurt you. That's for the pirates."

Pirates? "Prove it then." Madge nodded at the dagger. It was a risky move, but he knew her name, seemed to know Grandma Wendy too. How long had he been stalking her? "Give it to me."

"I like you, Madge." Grinning, he untied the dagger and tossed it to her.

She caught the dagger one-handed and pointed it at his chest. "Name."

"Peter Pan."

"Stupid name."

"No worse than Madge." He wrinkled his nose.

"How do you know me? My grandmother?"

"Bit of a long story."

"I've got all night."

"I have *forever.*"

Madge scoffed. "What the hell does that mean?"

He took a few steps forward until the tip of the blade touched his belly. He stood a few inches taller than Madge and seemed pleased by the fact. He patted her head.

She swatted at his arm. "Don't touch me."

He snickered.

"Listen, *Pan.* Whatever game you're working, I'm not interested. I don't have time for stupid magic tricks. So just—"

Pan wrapped his forearm around her neck, cutting her off mid-sentence. She gasped, gulping panicky breaths. He pried the dagger from her fingers with ease and held it at the tip of her nose, as though planning to cut it off. His breath was hot on her ear and smelled like old meat. She tried to turn away, but he wasn't having it.

"Margaret—"

"Madge," she spat.

"Madge, then. You're right. This is a game of sorts—not like any you've played. But you're also wrong because you *are* going to be interested when you hear what I have to say."

There was nothing on Earth he could say that would make her want to do anything but smash his tiny teeth in.

"I know you're on your way to where you think your mother is. But I've got news for you. Jane isn't in Chicago."

Except that.

Part of her knew he was trying to bait her. The other part didn't care.

"Where is she, then?"

He kissed her earlobe. "Secret."

She slammed her elbow back, aiming for his gut, but he turned out of the way, yanking her neck with him. They hit the ground, and Madge tried to kick free of his grasp. His legs were faster than hers. They clamped around her knees. Pinned.

"I like you, Madge, so I'm going to give you another chance to be civilized. I can't tell you where Jane is, but I can take you to her."

Her face tingled, and her teeth ground. "How do I know you're telling the truth?"

"You don't."

Something was wrong. Why did some freak on a power trip stalk her for weeks only to give her exactly what she wanted? All signs pointed to danger, but she ignored them. "I want your word that you're taking me to my mother. No funny shit."

He reached around her middle and placed something in her hand. She craned her neck over his arm to see. An acorn.

"What's this?"

"My word."

Freak. "Fine. Let me up."

"Are you going to run?"

"Thinking about it."

He hesitated then loosened his grip. He was on his feet in a blink and pulled her to standing. He watched her, eyes narrowed. It was like he wanted to chase her. She wouldn't give him the satisfaction. Besides, he was right. Pan had said the magic words. Madge was interested.

"You have a car or something?"

He scrunched his nose. "Why would I need a car to fly?"

She looked down. He hovered a few inches from the ground, arms out in a grand "ta-da" gesture. "How are you doing that? Strings? Magnets?" She threw a stick under his feet, which rolled through without a problem. "Mirrors?"

"I told you already."

"Right." She rolled her eyes. "Pixie dust."

"Precisely."

Pan reached into a pouch at his hip and flung something like dirt on her.

It stung her eyes and flew up her nose. She gagged.

"Happy thoughts, Madge."

She tried to shake it off, but the stuff clung like wet glitter. She coughed until her throat ached, dragging her nails across her tongue.

"You're not thinking happy thoughts." He tapped his foot, head tilted. "It's not hard."

Know what'd make me happy? Punching you in that smug little—

And she was airborne, shoved from the sidewalk like her feet and the ground were opposite poles of a magnet. Her stomach rolled, and her body lurched from side to side, unable to stabilize. Pan grabbed her hand and pulled her higher.

The ground raced away. The sidewalk was a squiggly line in the distance. Cars were the size of Hot Wheels. Wind tangled her hair and smacked her face. Soon, her nose was numb.

"Where are we going?" she shouted over the roar of the whipping wind.

He pointed to a pair of stars up ahead. "Second star to the right and straight on 'til morning."

"What does that mean? You can't fly to a star."

Peter Pan laughed.

Michael woke, gagging. He spat the ball of whiskey phlegm into a glass and sat up, cradling his head to keep it from falling off of his neck. He was too old for this, or so his doctor said, but no amount of anti-anxiety meds had ever been able to lurch him straight into the land of dreamless sleep the way a tumbler of spirits could. Anyway, Michael *was* too old to keep up the charade that living a healthy lifestyle would put off the hand of death. Bloody eighty years old, he was. It was like being taunted, tortured to keep living while the others... If only he had the courage to...

No. Mustn't think like that. There's still hope, after all. There's still Margaret.

He sighed and lurched his creaking body to a semi-standing position. His knee locked, and for a minute, Michael was trapped against the chair. His brain was still a little soupy from drink, and he blinked several times to keep the spins at bay.

Several seconds passed before he was able to take a tentative step. He moved cautiously, using furniture as handholds into the kitchen. The aftermath of his binge looked like a damn murder scene. He vowed to wake up early and clean it up before Margaret saw. Poor girl didn't deserve to be subjected to his shortcomings.

"Fine guardian you're turning out to be, Michael," he slurred. "Damn good thing you never had kids, you miserable old fool." He stepped in a puddle of sticky red wine and slipped, missing the corner of the counter by millimeters. His head hit the tile with a loud crack that rang in his ears and traveled down the length of his body.

The last thing he heard before passing out was the sound of someone screaming.

From the Diary of Wendy Moira Angela Darling

Dearest Diary, I think I may die of happiness. Is that absurd? Of course it is, but here, none of that matters.

Here. That, in and of itself, is a loaded word. Where is here? It's Neverland! Yes, the very Neverland from my stories. It's exactly as I imagined except so much... more. In Neverland, flowers bloom in colors one has never before heard of. The yellows are gold, and the reds are fire, and the greens are lush and vibrant, and I could roll in the soft, blue grass forever. Writing it all down is a necessary injustice. I shall never want to forget these first moments and the ones that follow. I can't help feeling that this place—that boy—was created for me, by me. In fact, Peter Pan himself all but confirmed it.

"Come with me, Wendy," he said. (Were more beautiful words ever uttered?)

At first, I protested because that's what a proper lady does. A proper lady does not run off with a young man at the slightest hint of an invitation.

"What of my brothers? I can't leave them behind."

He approached the boys and examined them like a general examines new recruits, turned their heads this way and that, poked their soft, milk-fed bellies.

"Okay, Wendy. They can come."

The walls practically shuddered with our cheers.

He showered us with a sparkling dust that made Michael sneeze but felt warm on my skin. Peter held my hand, and I wished he would never let go.

And then, dearest Diary, we flew.

Second star to the right, straight through until morning. We arrived, greeted by the brightest sun and warmest air.

Tonight, there was a feast in our honor. The food was unconventional—what should one expect in the middle of a mystical island?—but not unappetizing. John ate very little—his stomach upsets for days after traveling—and Michael devoured everything that was put in front of him. It pleased Peter, which pleased me. I shall remember to give Michael something special.

After dinner, Peter insisted on a hunt. Pirates had come ashore and were looking to steal precious healing flowers from Pan's garden. (How exciting! Pirates!) Being a proper lady, I didn't ask to join, though secretly I wished they would let me come along.

"You must wait for us here, Mother," Peter said. "Prepare our medicine for bedtime."

He's taken to calling me Mother, a fact I found disappointing until he named himself Father. We shall be like husband and wife!

"Of course," I said. "Be safe, my fearsome warrior."

And then—just as the Lost Boys had rounded the bend into the deepest part of the forest—Peter leaned in (he smelled of trees and light and sweet berries) and kissed me gently on my cheek.

I decided at that moment that I should like to stay in Neverland forever.

Chapter Five

Once upon a time...

JAMES HOOK, CAPTAIN OF THE *Jolly Roger*, pillager of worlds, the most fearsome pirate of the seven seas, had set out with a gleam in his eye and the taste of fortune on his tongue. Somewhere out there was the rumored Fountain of Youth, a lagoon with waters said to keep a man young and powerful forever. Months he'd spent on the water. Years. Abandoned by half his crew and hated by the others, Hook refused to give up his search.

One day, after riding out the worst storm he'd seen in a decade, the *Jolly Roger* happened upon a lagoon with water the color of purest blue, so clean one could see clear to the bottom. As the ship plowed through its waves, Hook had spotted a group of boys wading along the shore. The tallest of them flew—like a bloody bird—and landed on the deck of the ship. He called himself Pan, Lord knew why. Pan, as Hook understood, was a hoofed creature, half-goat, half something else. The boy was like a cherub, blond and pale, with eyes the color of chocolate.

"Welcome to Neverland," the boy had said.

Hook asked why it was called that.

"Because this is where boys go to never grow up."

Hook had nearly collapsed with joy. He'd found it! The famed lagoon! He would barrel up as much of the water as the *Jolly Roger* could carry and then set off for home.

All that seemed a lifetime ago. It was like the ship was anchored to the very earth. It wouldn't move. Hook and his crew were trapped in Neverland.

As time went on, it became clear that Pan was the leader of their little boy troop. Hook didn't dislike him. A capable leader, Pan knew when to strike and when to stroke his followers—all except his first mate, a boy called Peter.

Dark-haired and demon-eyed, Peter didn't trust Hook. Didn't trust any of the crew. It was only fair, Hook supposed. He didn't trust Peter either. Unrest shifted beneath the boy's tanned skin. Today, it was more like a hurricane.

It was noon or as close to noon as Hook could determine. It was impossible to measure the day by hours, and so he looked to the sun to orient himself. The Lost Boys—Pan's name for his men—came to the shore with supplies for Hook's crew. Food, wood for their stoves. Pan sympathized with their plight and offered comfort while they searched for a means of escape.

"Any meat today?" Hook asked as the boys boarded the *Jolly Roger*.

"A few rabbits." Pan shrugged. "Somethin' messed with our traps."

"Or they weren't set right." Peter shot a look at one of the boys, a small, dark thing with twin scars along his chin.

Pan patted the dark boy's shoulder. "They were set up fine."

Rabbits? Squirrels, more like. Yesterday, it was a pig with hardly enough meat to fill a child's belly. Hook heard the men's grumbling and saw the way they huddled at the stern with hushed voices. There'd be mutiny next. Hook would not have a mutiny on his ship.

"It's not enough." He tossed the rabbits at Pan's feet. "This is pathetic. I thought yer boys were hunters."

"They are," Pan said.

The boys nodded sheepishly.

Peter's face reddened. His fists shook at his sides. "Seriously?"

Pan knelt to pick up the rabbits, and Peter kicked him, hard, in the side. Rage flared, kick after kick. Pan didn't fight back, though, and that intrigued Hook. Pan curled into himself, blood spurting from his nose and mouth. The Lost Boys cheered Peter on with no concern for their leader. Hook's trollish crew wandered out from below deck, blinking against the harsh light of day. A few salivated at the sight of spilled blood. Even Smee's eyes glittered red.

Peter kicked even after Pan stopped moving. Stopped breathing. He kicked and jabbed until bones broke and flesh tore, until the boy Pan was little more than a human stain on Hook's deck.

And then Peter stopped, and a thick silence fell over the ship. Hook's fingers grazed the hilt of his sword. He almost wanted the little pillock to try something stupid.

"Get off my ship," Hook said. "And take your filthy little vermin with you."

Peter smiled, licking a drop of crimson that'd splashed onto his lip. He turned to the Lost Boys, fist in the air. "I am the Pan now!"

Cheers.

Hook's men shifted their weight. A cloud of tension settled over the *Jolly Roger*. Gone were the thoughts of empty bellies. Only a thirst for excitement remained. Hook grinned. This was what the men needed: a good, old-fashioned slaughter. So what if they were mere boys? They dealt with demons. With magic. Pixies.

Peter wrenched a golden sword from the hilt at the dead Pan's belt. He thrust it in Hook's direction.

Please do, Hook thought.

"Neverland declares war on your pirates, Hook. Enjoy your last night. Tomorrow, you and your men die."

Hook withdrew his sword and grazed the edge of the blade against Pan's. "You first."

Peter grinned and leapt from the ship, flying into the sun like a thunderbird.

Chapter Six

MADGE WASN'T REALLY FLYING. IT was impossible.

"You'll learn, Madge," Pan shouted over the sound of the breeze. "Nothing is impossible if you have enough imagination."

He pulled her higher into the sky, picking up speed. Cool air turned frigid, and Madge shivered. Ice laced her eyelashes. She blinked it away. Objects below became too small to see. If she fell, she'd not only die, but her body would be obliterated—a smear of red across the asphalt for the paperboy to find during his morning rounds. Madge reached up with her other hand to take Pan's arm. Rather than holding on, he let go, a grim smile on his face.

For an instant, she hovered. Then her stomach dropped to her feet, and she fell, arms flailing, reaching for anything. A scream froze in her chest.

It felt like she'd fallen a thousand miles before he finally caught her around her waist. She took long, shaky breaths before she could speak. "What's wrong with you? I almost died!"

"It's a game, Madge. Don't you like games?"

Her head spun. More games. She got the feeling his games only got worse.

He winked. "Look up."

She obeyed because the only other choices were down and forward at his face, and she had no interest in either.

"That star to your right, the brightest one? That's Neverland."

Neverland. Flying boys. She was hallucinating. It was the only explanation. Someone had drugged her, and this was the result.

Speed rocked her body as they shot upward. She could barely keep her head steady. Pan's laughter vibrated in her chest, and she squeezed her eyes shut, willing it to be over, willing herself to wake up.

He pinched her back, hard. "You're missing it!"

Madge didn't care.

A bright light pierced her eyelids, and warmth enveloped her body. She opened one eye, but all she saw was white, like staring directly into the sun for too long. Pan's grip loosened, but she refused to relinquish hers. She wouldn't fall for that again. He tried to wriggle out of her hold, but her arms formed a vise around his middle.

"You can let go," he said.

"Screw you."

"You won't fall. I promise."

"Like I'm gonna believe you."

"Would you just look down, girl?" He said *girl* like an insult.

She hesitated before finally looking down. They were about a foot above the ground. Sneering, she let go of Pan and landed gently on a bed of deep, blue grass that seemed to bend away from her step.

Pan puffed out his chest, hands perched on his waist. "Madge Darling, welcome to Neverland."

Neverland. It seemed a hodgepodge of landscape ripped from a dream. Or maybe a nightmare. On one side, lush forest grew dense with heat and energy. Flowers bloomed in a rainbow of colors. They shuddered as Madge gazed at them, and then, as Pan looked in their direction, shriveled to pale, dry nothings. On the other side, there was snow, a round hill of it, smooth and sparkling. She wanted to touch it. As she approached, the hill caved at the center, and a rush of arctic air blew. Something growled. She froze.

Large, pointed ears, followed by silvery fur and teeth the length of Madge's hand, emerged from the hole in the center of the snow hill slowly. The creature's eyes were black and rimmed in gold. Madge held her breath. Stepped back. She didn't even like small, manageable animals, let alone ones that looked at her as a midafternoon snack.

Pan's hand clamped around her arm and pulled her away. "Snowball doesn't like to be bothered during the day."

"Snowball?" Madge hissed. "The thing's name is frigging *Snowball*?"

"Fitting, isn't it? Poor thing needs his beauty rest." Pan made a kissy face at the creature. "Nighty-night, Snowball."

Snowball licked his massive chops with a long purple tongue and yawned. Madge saw clear down his throat, wide enough to swallow her whole. As he turned, his tail flicked a bank of snow, which hit Madge dead in the face.

Pan let out one explosive *ha* and crumpled over, shoulders shivering in silent giggles.

"Damn cat," she muttered.

Some of the snow dripped into her mouth. It tasted smoky and sweet, like burnt sugar.

"Best not to eat too much," Pan said. "That's how Snowball tracks you."

He led her away from the snow and into the jungle. Roots rippled in the ground as if trying to trip her. Pan danced a jig through their talons while Madge struggled to stay upright. She leaned on a gnarled tree trunk to regain her balance only to be smacked away by one of the branches.

"She groped me!" The tree's voice was like a whistle through the branches, high-pitched, fast, and almost impossible to hear.

"Talking trees. Okay." Madge stuffed her hands in her pockets. *Trapped in the Wizard of frigging Oz. If the Wicked Witch shows up, I'm out.*

Pan's eyes twinkled. "There's more."

Deeper into the jungle, the foliage grew bigger—trees, taller, leaves the size of her face. They dwarfed her. A squawk echoed from somewhere in the branches. Soon, the whole canopy erupted in trills, but Madge didn't see any of the birds.

"Neverbirds," Pan said. "Bad omen to see one."

"Why?"

"Because you can never be too sure if it's a bird or a girl." He licked his lips. "I saw someone shoot one once."

"Which was it? Bird or girl?"

He grinned.

She chanced a glance upward and thought she spotted the flick of a blue tail feather. Sound pulsed all around her, and she couldn't put a name to any of it. After seeing Snowball, her imagination ran wild with fanged squirrels and sharp-clawed rabbits ready to sink their teeth into her neck. She wasn't going to stay here any longer than necessary.

"You said you'd bring me to my mother."

Pan shushed her. "This way."

An opening in the trees led to a kind of forest room. Pebbles that shone like opals dotted the ground. At the far side was a lily, the bloom the size of Madge's head, its petals bright except at the center. Red dots speckled the inner part of the petals like blood splatters. Madge stepped closer, reaching out to stroke the velvety petals.

Pan's hand clamped down on her wrist. "You don't want to do that."

"Why not? It's beautiful."

"So is a shark before it bites your head off."

She snorted. "It's a flower."

"Watch."

He pulled her back, away from the flower. A hummingbird flitted from the copse of trees to her left. Its feathers glittered blue and green in the sunlight as it thrummed between flowers, tucking its tiny head between the petals.

"Watch," Pan repeated.

The hummingbird seemed to consider the blood lily a moment before diving into its center. The petals shivered to life and folded over the bird. There was a strangled squeal and a sickening pop. When the lily opened again, new red dots glittered at its center.

"See?" Pan grinned.

Madge couldn't take her eyes off the lily. She imagined the body of the hummingbird being passed down the thick stem like a mouse through a snake and choked back a gag. "God, is everything in this place going to try to kill me?"

Pan shrugged. "Not *everything.*"

"Where the hell am I? Are we even on earth? Did I die?"

He gestured grandly, open-handed, like a game-show host. "I told you. Neverland. Short for Never, Never Land. I came up with the name myself."

"Neverland. I don't get it."

"Neverland is a place where children *never* grow up."

"Never?"

"Never, never." Pan winked.

"Impossible. Everyone grows up."

"Were you always this stupid?"

"Excuse me?"

"Impossible, impossible," he mocked her voice. "You think everything is impossible. Only idiots think things are impossible."

Madge opened her mouth, but before she could get anything out, Pan stuffed a fistful of leaves in it. She coughed and lashed out with her fists, but he was oblivious to her anger, pacing around her, gesticulating wildly. "Look around you, girl. This whole place is *impossible*, but it's here, isn't it? You're standing on real ground on a real island that *really* is Neverland."

He pointed to a subtle path in the grass. "This path leads to the mermaid lagoon. This"—he marched to another path—"leads to the old Red Man camp on the opposite side of the island. No more Red Men there, though. These others"—Pan spun—"lead everywhere else and nowhere and back again."

A growl erupted from somewhere behind her, and she jumped. "What the hell was that?"

"Those," Pan said, "would be my men."

He leaped into the air, cupping his hands to his mouth, and crowed loud and long. A flock of bright-red birds swirled from the tops of the trees like a tornado of caws and feathers.

Madge backed away from him, a voice in her head demanding that she run. She tripped over a thick root. Several pairs of small hands reached out to grab her. Dirty fingers snatched the hood of her sweater and jammed it over her face, tying the cords around her neck.

"To the house!" Pan called.

Madge clawed at the hood, unable to get any kind of useful grip before the hands were all over her, carrying her. Branches smacked her face and neck, and fingers dug into her waist and shoulders. She screamed for help, but the creatures shouted over her. What had she gotten herself into?

Chapter Seven

FROM THE MOMENT PETER PAN left Neverland to the moment he returned, Hook's gaze was turned skyward. Being dead, the fierce sunlight didn't bother him. It was well past midday when Pan returned—as it was always well past midday when Pan left—and the sky quaked as he broke through the clouds. He wasn't alone.

Hook sighed.

"Problem, Cap'n?" Smee poked at a toy boat assembled from tree bark and a banana leaf as it drifted along the edge of the lagoon.

"He's brought a girl with him."

Smee frowned convincingly, though his ghostly eyes were vacant.

"He's going to do it again."

"Mutiny." Smee shook his head. "Right shame."

"Not mutiny. Murder."

"Same, same."

Hook nodded. "Aye."

It wasn't the inevitable that bothered him, though. The dead didn't have the luxury of worry. The dead couldn't anticipate the worst because it'd already happened. It was the question of Hook's role in all of this that made him uneasy. Bystander? He'd had enough of that to fill a thousand lifetimes. Tiger Lily would want to know, if she didn't already.

Even from a distance, the girl in Pan's grip looked disturbingly familiar, like an apparition from a past life.

Smee looked up from his boat and chuckled. "Look, Cap'n. Wendy's back."

Wendy. Of course.

The girl was most likely a relative. Not a daughter—Jane had been and gone. Granddaughter? Even with all he'd seen in his life, it was hard for Hook to imagine someone as youthful and vibrant as Wendy as a grandmother. He'd had high hopes for her. Pan had been smitten. Any oaf could see it. But Pan was a shark of a different color. His feelings for Wendy only turned his heart black. Black by a pirate's standards was a chasm of unfathomable darkness, as Hook could attest. Lost his hand because of it, didn't he? A hook for Hook.

No. A bystander he would not be, for it was time that Pan was made to pay for what he'd done.

"Smee. Pack up the ship. We're heading inland."

Smee pulled the toy boat from the lagoon with a groan. "But *he's* inland, sir."

"That's the point. We've some pirating to attend to."

Smee clapped his ghostly hands, smashing the boat between them. "Shipwreck," he mumbled.

Chapter Eight

THEY QUESTIONED MICHAEL FOR HOURS. What exactly had he heard? What was his relationship like with Margaret? With Wendy? How often did he see them? Had he ever had any inappropriate thoughts about his niece?

He rubbed the calloused ends of his missing digits as they threw accusation after accusation in his face. But Michael didn't answer any of them. He couldn't. His thoughts were too loud to make it through to his voice without killing him. Michael didn't have to have seen it to know. Pan had taken Margaret.

Wendy didn't know. Wouldn't ever know if Michael had his way. If the heart failure didn't kill her, that would. Bad enough when Jane... His stomach rolled with whiskey rot. How did he let himself get like this?

"Mr. Darling? Mr.—Christ, can we get this guy some coffee or something? He's smashed."

Smashed. What an excellent word. Yes, that's exactly what Michael was: smashed and twisted and un-bloody-recognizable.

The detective was talking, but Michael didn't care. They'd never find her. He rolled his forehead on the table. It was cool against his hot face. *Still talking. Shut up.* He closed his eyes and lay still, drifting into sleep, and dreamed about his last night in Neverland.

"You're mine," Pan had said.

And Wendy hadn't argued.

Michael waited for her to fight for them, to defend him as he'd defended her against the pirates. His fingers still wept blood, long after

Pan declared them healed. They would never be healed. Michael would never be healed. Pan had taken the Darlings and would never give them back.

Everything hurt. The back of her head throbbed in time to the sound of stomping. When they finally unwrapped the hood from her face, she saw Pan reclined over the arms of a horned throne, a wood flute to his lips. He caught her looking at him and stood.

"No." Madge scrambled backward, scraping her hand on bits of bark and rock. "Stay away from me, you freak."

"Why so cruel, Madge?" He smiled.

"You hit me!"

Pan twirled the flute between his fingers. "I did no such thing. They did."

She turned. Behind her, a group of monsters, at least a dozen, stood on human legs with thick fur covering their feet. Their heads were patchworks of teeth and hair and animal faces. The one at the center had the face of a tiger with long, sharp teeth in all the wrong places. It crouched close to Madge and growled.

Pan's laughter jarred the fear in her chest. "Okay, okay, boys. That's enough. Off with your heads so you can properly welcome our distinguished guest, Madge Darling."

Boys? Yes, after the patchwork masks were removed, they looked more like boys. Kind of. Their faces were caked with dirt except where bright-pink scars showed through. More than one of them was missing an ear. The one with the tiger face smiled, revealing incisors sharpened to points. The smallest of the group struggled to extricate his head from his wolf mask then donned a black top hat.

Drawn by fear and curiosity, Madge studied them as they studied her. They seemed to be caught somewhere between boys and that time when voices changed and hair grew in places you didn't know it could. Their bodies were small but muscular and carried the ripe stench of sweat and sour milk like babies left to sit in formula-soaked onesies.

Pan stepped between Madge and the boys, and they automatically fell in line beside him. Pan beamed. "These are my men. The Lost Boys."

She was surrounded, and it felt like one of those old "This Could Be You" videos where the girl was passed out in the middle of the frat house, and the guys... They'd pass her around like a toy.

Madge scrambled for a sharp rock and brandished it like a blade. "Don't you dare touch me."

They all looked at her with mixed expressions. Pan seemed amused until Tiger-Faced Boy stepped forward. "Aw, Pan, see? I told you girls can't take this kind of game. Now she'll be blubberin' all day."

Pan wheeled on him, fist raised, and then changed his mind. "Fine, Slightly. If you're such an expert on *girls*, why don't you show the little lady around while the men and I check the traps."

"But I—come on, Pan, you can't—"

Pan put his hand up. The conversation was over. "Up and out, boys. March!" He turned to Madge and winked. "We shall return with a feast fit for you, lady."

"You can't just leave me here!" Madge said. "You promised to bring me—hey!"

Thrusting a fist in the air, Pan led the boys into a hole in the wall, their chants echoing long after they'd gone.

"This is unbelievable." Madge stood, mumbling and dusting the dirt off her pants. "I'm an idiot. Should've just waited for a cab or something."

The one called Slightly kicked a rock in the direction of the hole then spit. "Right then, *girl*. Let's get this over with."

"Get what over with?"

Slightly rolled his eyes and pointed to the tunnel. "You heard him. I have to show you things."

Now that the room was clear, Madge realized they'd brought her somewhere underground. Roots wove through the walls. Weeds grew in the corners, sprouting plain, white flowers. Slightly grabbed her elbow and pulled. After two steps, the room spun, and she nearly collapsed on top of him.

"Tootles is a bit heavy-handed with the club," Slightly said. "Usually, he's knocking out rabbits, a wild pig or two..."

Madge glared. "Do I look like a friggin' wild pig?"

Slightly grinned.

"Shut up." She glanced toward the tunnel door where Pan and

the others had gone. She tried to decide if Slightly could outrun her. *Probably could.*

She ran her hand over the back of her head, where a lump the size of an egg had formed. Her fingers came away sticky. "I probably have a concussion or something."

Slightly shrugged.

"I need a bandage. A rag. Something."

He rolled his eyes, muttered something about girls, then disappeared inside a small cubby tucked beneath a bunk. He returned holding a small orange leaf.

Madge raised an eyebrow.

"Medicine leaf." He tore it open, and clear juice oozed out. "See?"

"It looks disgusting."

"Honestly."

Slightly shoved her head forward and dabbed some of the juice on the wound. It stung at first but then felt pleasantly warm, and the throb in her head and neck waned.

"Thanks."

He smiled out of the corner of his mouth. Madge noticed a dimple so deep it could've been carved out with a spoon. It made his overall appearance less menacing.

Without the distraction of pain, she was able to think. Her bag. What'd they do with it? A brief scan of the room and she spotted it shoved behind Pan's chair. She dug through it. Everything seemed to be accounted for except the peanut butter—though the empty jar wasn't far away—and Grandma Wendy's book.

She glared at Slightly. "Did you take it?"

"Take what?"

"My book."

"I don't care about any book. Now come on."

Strapping her bag tightly over her shoulders, she followed him toward another tunnel in the wall.

"This way is out. So when you need to do your business..." Slightly pantomimed spraying from a hose.

"Ew."

"Just stay away from the red thorn bush. Once they're in you, they don't come out."

Madge wondered how long a person could hold it before they died. A day? Two? She had a strong bladder. She could do it.

The tunnel was so small that they had to drag themselves by the elbows. The floor of the tunnel was like one long rumble strip, helping the climbers to gain enough traction to propel their bodies forward without slipping back. It was dark, so Madge had to rely on the sound of Slightly's breathing. The air became hot and difficult to breathe the further away from the room they crawled.

"Are we almost there?"

"Don't get your knickers in a bunch. We're nearly there."

Slightly grunted, and she heard his fist hit something solid, and then the tunnel was flooded with light. Madge followed him up to the opening where he climbed out then offered his hand. "Watch your step. You'll have to find a sturdy branch."

She wrenched herself from the tunnel and balanced on the edges. It was a tree—taller than any tree she'd ever seen and as wide as a house. The branches twisted together to form crude bridges. Knots were carved deep enough to be chairs. Madge could see for miles. Green jungle in all directions—Snowball's snow hill there, toward the center—punctuated by bursts of blue and gold and purple. Beyond that, ocean. Blue-green water that sparkled as it waved. At the far end of the island, the gaping mouth of a volcano swallowed a cloud. From this angle, a girl could almost forget all the nightmares Neverland held.

"Don't tell Pan I brought you up here," Slightly said.

"Why?"

"Outsiders aren't supposed to know how to find the tree house until they've been initiated."

"Initiated?" Madge's stomach fell. "What's that mean?"

"It means you're in the club, not that you'd ever get in, being a girl and all. Just. You know." His tone was pleading, and he looked down, fiddling with his thumb. She noticed a chunk of it was missing.

"Okay. I won't."

Slightly sighed, relieved.

"So why did you bring me?"

He crossed his arms. "Because everyone ought to see this. Even girls."

She shook her head. The way this boy talked about girls—like Pan did—like girls were lesser creatures... Madge thought the cootie phase was supposed to end in elementary school.

"Well, thanks. It's... nice."

It was hard to tell beneath the grit, but Madge thought she saw Slightly blush.

Chapter Nine

PETER PAN KNEW EVERYTHING THERE was to know about the jungle. He could read the pattern of stripes on a tiger's back just by the sound of leaves crunching under its paws. He could predict within seconds the first drops of rain that would hit the ground, where and how much and for how long it would rain. He even knew the boys better than they knew themselves. Why wouldn't he? He'd been watching them since they were born.

Girls, though. Girls were a puzzle to Pan. There was little Peter Pan hated more than not knowing.

It's not my fault, though, he thought. Wendy was so… *accommodating*. How was he to know that Madge was so… not?

No. Definitely not my fault.

At least all of his traps had worked. Curly's, so far, had been empty. They were always empty. Not surprising, though, considering Curly was a few tail feathers short of a turkey. But what could he say? The boy made Pan feel better when things didn't seem to be going his way.

He let Curly mull over his latest failure—a box propped up on a stick—and took a moment to listen to the wind for signs of the Red Men. Since the chief died and Tiger Lily took it upon herself to don her father's ceremonial headdress, declaring herself Chief, the troop had been antsy. Those who wouldn't take their anger out on Tiger Lily directed it toward Pan and his men. Pan usually welcomed a fight, but only on his terms.

Tootles tapped Pan's shoulder. "You thinkin', Pan?"

He nodded.

"Oh." Tootles took a step back, but Pan felt his newest recruit's eyes on the back of his head. Not one of his best choices, adopting Tootles at such a young age. Tootles would last longer than the others, but would never grow out of the nursery stage.

Pan sighed. "What is it?"

"I just wanted to say sorry for hitting Madge so hard. I wasn't thinkin'. Just swingin'." He swung his club through the air in a crude reenactment.

Inside, Tootles was soft. On the outside, though… Pan smiled reassuringly and patted his arm. "No harm done, my good man." Every army had room for the boys who did the swinging.

Erratic footsteps crunched through the north jungle, echoing into their path. Pan and the boys leaped to attention. Pan expertly pulled his dagger from its sheath. The sound was too haphazard to be a Red Man. A new pirate, perhaps? The mermaids had promised Pan a new ship, and they'd yet to deliver.

The figure fought through a tangle of vines before tumbling at Pan's feet.

"Nibs." Pan stepped on the side of the boy's head, keeping his face close to the mud. "What have I told you about keeping quiet during the hunt?"

"But, Pan—"

"Not that I would care if you got scalped by the rogues."

Nibs's reply was muffled by the mud slowly seeping into his mouth and nose.

"What's that?" Pan chuckled, motioning for the others to laugh as well. "Can't quite hear you."

Nibs struggled to push himself out of the mud, his arms flailing out and barely missing Pan's leg. He stepped harder on the boy's head.

"Did you say you were a pile of snot, Nibs?"

He nodded frantically.

"Did you say you were a…" Pan paused, thinking. "A pile of stinking pig dung?"

He nodded again, and his back spasmed. Pan rolled his eyes and finally let Nibs up. He gagged as the mud dripped from his nose and nearly puked. When he finally caught his breath, Nibs said, "I found a live one."

They followed Nibs north, over another of Tootles's woefully empty traps—this one a pile of leaves over a shallow hole. Deep within a tangle of trees, flies buzzed excitedly. Pan recognized the trap immediately as one of his own. The business end of Pan's trap plunged through the pig just as it was designed to do, but because it was such a large animal, the spear had missed a few internal organs. Blood drained from the gash in its side, its pinky flesh gaping open. Its eyelids fluttered, and its breaths came short and quick.

Pan dropped to his knees in front of the animal. *Beautiful.* He pinched the pig's eyes open, savoring the flash of fear before they dulled again. Keeping his gaze locked with the pig's, Pan dipped his fingers into the wound and licked the blood from them. *I am a warrior, the greatest of all warriors, never to be defeated.*

The pig let out its final breath, and Pan inhaled it. "Wrap it carefully, and keep it separate from the other catches," he told Nibs. "This one is for Madge."

From the diary of Wendy Moira Angela Darling

It's hard to believe that a place as strikingly beautiful as Neverland is fertilized by so much blood.

The pirates are dead. I hold no loyalty to them, but the sight of my boys returning (yes, Diary, MY boys) covered in the blood and mud of battle nearly tore the breath from my chest. My heart fell into my stomach, and I feared they'd been hurt.

"I killed the parrot!" Michael said—baby Michael, who would always name every animal he saw during our daily walks in the park.

"How... wonderful?" I said.

Peter emerged, almost unrecognizable with the amount of gore on his body. (Does it make me terrible, Diary, that I still found him beautiful?) He danced in the blood trickling from his hands and encouraged the others to do the same. I clapped in time to their disjointed rhythm.

Do not think me bad, Diary. As Mother, I cannot disappoint Father. It is my duty to obey and love and cherish without judgment, something my own mother could take a lesson in. I danced with my adopted family in the blood of the vicious, ruthless pirates.

Later, when the boys were asleep and the night was still, Peter let me bathe him. I insisted, of course, not just for the sake of cleanliness (the smell of blood permeated quickly), but because it was my duty.

I'm growing (well, not anymore, I suppose) into a young woman. Before Peter's rescue, I was reaching an age when talk of my future began. My marriageability. Mother pulled me aside one night after a particularly rousing party downstairs and insisted she tell me everything she knew about keeping a husband happy. She even had one picked out for me—an intelligent but hopelessly soft boy named Gerald.

"Gerald will have needs, my dear."

"Such as?" I asked.

And she told me. "You mustn't be frightened, pet," she said once she'd finished describing an act so foul I insisted on washing myself after hearing of it.

I told her I wasn't frightened, but Diary, I was mortified.

That is, until I met Pan.

Peter allowed me to undress him, though (bless him) he seemed confused by the whole thing.

"We bathe in the ocean," he said. "When it's necessary."

"It's too dark."

He smiled (Lord, that smile), and the sunrise peeked through the branches of the tree house. My Peter, master of the night and day in Neverland.

I insisted he stop—think of the boys!—and once again, the sun dipped.

Using a bundle of soft banana leaves as a sponge, I wiped the blood from Peter's body. I noticed a small sprouting of hair around his manhood (not at all as terrifying a thing as I had imagined) and said as much.

He lashed out at me, shoving me into the bunk, and I thought for a terrifying instant that this was how we would consummate our union—with anger instead of love. But he only covered himself and flew away.

Chapter Ten

BACK INSIDE THE TREE HOUSE, Slightly showed Madge where she would sleep. The long, narrow root with the center carved out and lined with moss was more like a coffin than a bed.

"Hopefully you'll fit," he said.

"And if I don't?"

"Pan will have to make adjustments."

She raised an eyebrow. "And that's... bad?"

Slightly crossed his arms and absentmindedly rubbed his sides. Before he could say anything, the echo of Pan and his troops drifted through the main tunnel. At first, their chanting was garbled, but as they approached, Madge realized they were singing a kind of gospel to Pan:

"... so crook your arm and place to brow,
Forward, boys, forward now!
'Tis the wise and strong that knows
None compare to Pan who crows!"

At the sight of Pan, all the boyishness Madge had seen in Slightly's face while at the top of the tree melted away. He clicked his heels. Saluted.

Pan ignored him and sauntered up to Madge, wearing a "wait until I show you" smile. "All settled in there, girl?"

"Actually, I—"

"Fantastic. Look here. I've brought you a gift."

The boys approached with large sacks over their shoulders. The tall one who had hit her dumped a sack at her feet, the bottom of it soaked in red. A pink snout poked out from the opening.

"Open it," Pan said.

Madge didn't consider herself squeamish, but the metallic smell of the blood hit her like a hammer, and it was a struggle not to gag. Covering her mouth and nose, she kicked the fold of the sack.

Bile rose up her throat and burned her nose. Before her was a mutilated pig; the ears were missing, and one of the eyes hung by a long strip of muscle, dangling close to its gaping mouth. This was what passed as a gift in Neverland?

"It's…"

"Nice one, Pan," Slightly said.

"I know," Pan said excitedly. "It will make a fitting feast."

Madge's stomach clenched as a fly crawled from the snout. "You expect me to eat this?"

Pan ignored her. "Lads, we've a lady to entertain. Get to work."

The boys scattered like spiders, their limbs flailing, grabbing things off makeshift shelves and out of cubbies. Madge tried to catch Slightly's eye, but he was as caught up in the chaos as the rest of them.

Pan hovered above it all, his unwavering gaze unnerving her like a housecat eyeing a bird from behind a window. As he drifted toward her, though, his face softened. He turned so that he looked at her upside down and chuckled. "While they're preparing dinner, do you want to go on a little adventure?"

"An adventure?"

"Yep." Pan offered his hand. "A little one."

Madge's thoughts turned to Snowball. The death lily. "What kind of adventure?"

"Does it matter?"

No, she told herself. It didn't. Because, yeah, there were things out there that could kill her, but wasn't that the same anywhere? Since coming to Neverland, a feeling had planted itself in her, like a laugh caught in the middle of her tongue. She was here to find her mother, and there was no doubt in her mind that she would. But the longer she looked into Pan's sparkling green eyes, the quieter that desire became.

After all, she had time. An entire island devoted to the dreams of kids... how could she not throw herself at it? Didn't she deserve this?

Madge smacked his hand away. "Race ya." She bolted for the tunnel and out into the open air. Pan chased after her, leaping into the air as soon as the tunnel ended. She reached up, and he grabbed her hands, pulling her into the sky.

They flew east toward a dense part of the jungle where the tops of the trees packed together like a lattice. Branches wove tightly between the branches of other trees, and moss dangled from the center of these clusters like chandeliers. Pan brought them down slowly into a small clearing and touched his finger to his lips. He mimed walking gently and took the lead. She followed, tiptoeing, wondering why they didn't just fly if walking made too much noise. But as the foliage grew denser around her, Madge realized it would be impossible to get through except on foot. And as the jungle closed around her, the light became sparser until it was too dark to see anything except Pan's silhouette. She reached out for him to guide her, but he moved too quickly.

"Peter," she whispered.

"Shush. This way."

"What way? I can't see you."

"Toward the light."

"What light? Oh."

Madge almost missed it—a flutter of light no bigger than her fist. It changed from gold to red to blue and back to gold again before disappearing into the brush. Keeping her eyes trained on the spot where it vanished, she inched forward. After a few steps, she almost tripped over Pan, crouched beside a fallen tree branch.

"What is it?" she asked.

"A fairy."

"But fairies aren't—"

Pan slapped his hand over her mouth before she could finish. "Don't you dare finish that sentence. If you do, you'll be a murderer."

Madge shook away his hand. "I don't see how—"

"Do shut up. You'll scare them away."

Whatever retort Madge had on the tip of her tongue stalled as hundreds of golden lights floated up from the brush. The rush of thousands of beating wings drowned the gentle hum of the sleeping jungle. The glow of their light trailed behind them as they flew higher, twirling around each other to create swirling vortexes of light that illuminated the ground. Drifting on the light was the soft chime of bells. One of them hovered close enough to see clearly—a tiny woman, naked except for a flower petal draped over her shoulders. The dainty thing reminded Madge of Thumbelina.

"They're singing," Madge said. The melody tugged at her heart. "I've heard this song before."

"All children know the fairy song," Pan whispered.

The tone of the melody changed, dipping deep into a minor key. Blurry images flashed through Madge's mind. They alternated between light and dark, joy and sorrow, until finally stopping on an image of the night sky, starless and cloudy. She gazed up past the lights and gasped.

The stars blinked out, one by one and then in great clusters. Pan held her hand as though to reassure her, but it didn't help. She'd seen the movies. She knew what it meant when the stars went out—the end of the world.

Pan's lips brushed her ear. "Relax. Just watch."

Madge wanted to pull away—having him this close to her felt wrong on an animal instinct level, like a sparrow flying close to a hawk—but she couldn't. His arm encircled her shoulders. She shuddered.

Just as the last star looked like it'd black out, it flickered and then shone brighter than even the hundreds of fairies together. It grew. It fell.

The fairies took off to meet it, and the vortex split, raining sparks like fireworks. Pan reached into his poncho and pulled out a small leather sack. He held it out and caught the few sparks he could reach.

When he finished, he showed it to Madge. "Fairy dust."

The sparks dulled until they became the sand-like stuff he'd thrown over her back home. She reached out to touch it. "What's it made of? Skin?"

Pan just smiled and stuffed the bag away.

Madge's neck and thighs started to cramp from crouching and staring upward, but she couldn't move, afraid that one misstep would disturb the fairies and destroy the display. The fairies spread out to create a kind of net. Their melody increased in tempo and volume until it was almost too loud to handle.

The star crashed into the fairy net, which cocooned around it.

The melody stopped.

The light dimmed, and the cocoon drifted in perfect unison between the trees and away from where Pan and Madge hid. Both held their breath until it was out of sight. Even with the fairies gone, their melody turned in the back of her mind, dredging through the muck of her past. She *had* heard it before.

It wasn't until they were trekking back toward the tree house that she remembered.

"My mother used to sing it to me. I don't know how I remember, but I do." Madge turned to Pan. "How did she know it?"

He shook his head.

"Don't shake your head. Tell me. You promised."

She saw Pan bite the inside of his cheek. A flutter of fury danced over his face before settling into calm passiveness. "What did you think of our adventure?"

A million thoughts passed through Madge's mind, all of them flashing red. He hadn't brought her here to keep promises. Then what did he bring her for? She couldn't begin to consider it. She broke into a trot, unable to run through the thick underbrush, back toward what she thought was the way to the tree house. She could just make out a faint opening when something huge and dark landed in her path.

It wasn't solid. The edges of the boy-shaped thing frayed, and she bet that if she tried to touch it, her hand would go straight through. Not that she would touch it. The shadow crackled like an electric current.

The shadow thrummed, unmoving. Even without eyes, it seemed to stare at her. She couldn't look away. Couldn't move. Her mind fogged, and her thoughts felt plucked from her mind until the only one left was: *Relax.*

Her muscles sagged. Her legs ached. Why had she run?

Pan stroked her shoulder. "Are you okay?"

She nodded.

They walked silently on.

Chapter Eleven

Once upon a time...

PETER, THE NEW PAN, DIDN'T come for Hook and his crew the next day. Or the next. Weeks passed. It seemed that Pan had found something else to occupy his time. As the crew ventured into the forests to forage and hunt, they returned with rumors of a peace treaty between Pan and the Red Men. Where the rumors came from, Hook didn't care to wonder. It wasn't what he'd expected to hear about the new leader of the Lost Boys. Blood and carnage, sure, but peace?

Hook suspected trickery.

With Pan distracted, though, it gave Hook and his crew time to search out a way to escape from the cursed island. The mermaids that lived in the lagoon's depths—terrifying creatures with skin like sharks and vicious teeth to match—had begun scratching at the hull. More than one of Hook's crew had been lured off the gangplank by their song. Different boys from Peter's crew arrived frequently, and Peter himself flew off to God knew where whenever he pleased. There *had* to be a way out.

One night, a Neverbird landed on the wheel with a message tied to its foot. Scratched on a bit of leather in dried mud was: *Meet tonite. Skull Rock. I will help yoo.*

Lost Boys, so lost they couldn't even write properly. Not that they cared. Their lives were that of games and things. In a small part of his heart, Hook envied them. But which one of the Lost

Boys had sent the message? Or was it just more trickery from Pan? Every glance from his crew now bore looks of contempt. They blamed Hook for it all and would sooner murder him than trust him. Hook had no choice. He had to take the risk.

Darkness came earlier than usual. Hook slipped over the side of the ship and into a rowboat, telling only his first mate, Smee, where he'd gone. He felt every one of his forty years as his arms strained against the chop. Skull Rock was just off the northern shore, out where the mermaids liked to take their food. The water splashed up the side of the boat, smelling of death and decay. Bits of bone and hair floated with the algae.

There was a protrusion on the side of Skull Rock that looked a little like a tooth and served as a tie-up for Hook's boat. He climbed over the jaw and into the mouth, patting his sword as a reassurance. Hook didn't normally kill children, but one could make an exception.

The mouth cave was dark and damp. Creepy-crawlies scratched the walls and skittered along the floor. Something cold brushed Hook's ankle, and he bit his tongue to keep from screaming.

"Oy," Hook said into the dark. "Come out. I don't like surprises."

A bell chimed, and a dainty light appeared, illuminating the whites of someone's eyes. As the light flitted across the face, Hook realized it was the little dark boy from the ship, the one Peter seemed to dislike so much.

"It's a fairy," the boy said, pointing to the light. "Tinker Bell's her name. I named her, 'cause of the way she talks like a bell."

Hook didn't give a rat's left eye about bells and fairies. "You said you could help."

The boy nodded.

"Help get us off the island?"

He nodded again.

Eloquent little blighter, wasn't he?

"Tell me how."

A shift in the darkness. Hook drew his sword as a tingle drifted down his spine. Something wasn't right.

"Now, boy!" Hook held the tip of the sword at the boy's eye level. "Tell me."

The boy's hands shook as he withdrew a stone from his pocket. It looked a simple pebble at first, but as the fairy's light shone on it, it sparkled like an opal. "Take this back to your ship. Have all your men touch it, and then tell it where you want to go. It'll steer you right."

Hook eyed the pebble. It didn't look magic. "You're sure."

"Uh-huh."

Hook expected the boy to toss the stone to him—the boy seemed to be very keen on getting rid of it—but instead, the boy held it in his open palm for Hook to take. Hook reached out, and a hiss sliced through the air. Pain rocketed up his arm, turning his stomach and blurring his vision.

Someone laughed.

"I did it, Pan!" the boy said. "I did just like you asked."

Hook fell against the wall of the cave, clutching his severed wrist. The hand was gone, kicked somewhere. He growled and slashed with his sword, hoping to hit something. Anything. His head swam, and he jabbed, feeling his blade stick into something soft.

Pan emerged from a hole in the cave wall, carrying a lantern. His golden sword was streaked with Hook's blood. He set the lantern down and picked up Hook's hand. The bone was shorn clean. Blood still dripped from it.

"Make a nice little treat for the crocodiles." Pan tossed the hand over the side of the rock and into the waves.

Hook clutched his wrist against his chest, wrapped tightly in the folds of his coat. His heart fluttered as he lost more and more blood. He would die here, at the feet of this *creature*.

Pan carried the lantern across the cave until it illuminated a lump on the ground: the boy, dead by Hook's sword. Pan looked from Hook to the boy and back again. "Two birds with one pebble, eh?"

"I'll kill you, Peter Pan," Hook swore through clenched teeth. "I promise you, if it's the last thing I do."

Pan's green eyes glittered in the light. "To die would be an awfully big adventure."

From the diary of Wendy Moira Angela Darling

Peter won't look at me. It's torture to watch him from my place on the other side of the tree house, away from the boys (more importantly, away from him!) and know that his love for me has faded.

What did I do wrong?   The only time he even acknowledges my presence is when I tell stories.

I've taken to filling the silences—few and far between as they are—with them. Cinderella, Snow White and Rose Red, Rumpelstiltskin… I've told them all so many times the boys mouth the words along with me. Once, as an attempted peace offering, I began telling one of Peter's stories, the one where he and the Red Men struck a peace treaty, so that each of them might live without interference from the other.

His face fell. "That's not what happened."

"I admit I wasn't there."

"No. You weren't. You don't know anything."

His words stung, but I wouldn't dare show it. I've learned much about him, and while he is erratic and inconsistent in most ways, in one he is steadfast. Predictable. Peter must always be forced to try harder. If one gives in, he loses interest.

I will never give in.

Chapter Twelve

MADGE HAD NEVER SEEN SO much food—if one could call it that—in one place in her entire life. The slaughtered pig was unrecognizable among the plates of chops and hunks of dripping meat. A platter of what looked like turkey legs sat at the center of the long table, surrounded by a blackened snake, the mouth of which was propped open with a stick. Its fangs gleamed white against the charred skin. Strange, star-shaped fruit spilled from bowls at the ends. Piles of various berries dotted the remaining surface. The boys stood behind the table with a bonfire roaring in the background, eyes fixed expectantly on her.

"It looks… uh, great," she said. "I guess."

In unison, they shifted their gaze to Pan, who nodded. Their chests deflated, relieved.

Pan sat at the head of the table and insisted Madge sit at the opposite end. The boys sprinkled themselves around the edges and slopped food into their mouths before she had a chance to pull out her chair. Pork juice splashed onto her cheek. Once at the zoo, Uncle Michael had forced her to watch a pair of wolves rip apart their lunch. This was like that, only with less grace.

A hand pushed a plate in front of her. Red and purple berries glistened on a bed of leaves. No meat. Madge wanted to thank whoever it was, but it was impossible to discern any one of the boys through the feeding frenzy. Pan watched it all, fingering a star fruit with a kind of grim satisfaction.

Madge was hesitant to put even the berries in her mouth. The guy was sick. He might've brought her all the way here to poison her—enslave her with his mind-control berries. A shadow twitched out of the corner of her eye. She rolled a small red berry between two fingers. It looked a little like a cherry. She cut a small slit in the side with her nail and sniffed the juice. Sweet, maybe a little bitter. What did poison even smell like? In the end, she decided that if Pan had wanted to kill her, he would have done it back on the street. Besides, her growling stomach argued that she hadn't eaten anything in forever, and the little brats had taken her peanut butter. If necessary, she'd sneak the granola bars from her bag when they weren't looking.

Madge popped the cherry-thing in her mouth and bit. It taste like a tomato rolled in sugar. Delicious. Three more went into her mouth without a thought. She got so caught up in eating the unusual berries in front of her that it took her a moment to notice the quiet. Cheeks packed with fruit, she glanced up and realized they were all staring at her. Her face warmed, and she sank back in the chair.

Pan leaned forward, inspecting the contents of her plate. "No meat?"

She shook her head, frantically chewing and swallowing.

"Hmm."

Out of the corner of her eye, Madge noticed Slightly fidgeting.

"I suppose it does take some getting used to. Not everyone can have an appetite like me." He raised his hands in a gesture of clearing the air, and the boys swiped the contents of the table to the ground, including Madge's half-finished dinner. "It's story time."

The boys cheered.

"Do you know any stories, girl?"

"I don't... uh..."

He scoffed. "Oh, come on. Everyone knows stories. Cinderella? Sleeping Beauty? Robin Hood?"

"Sure, yeah. I know them." Know *of* them, anyway.

"Excellent. Tell us a story."

Their stares felt like needles pressing into her skin. Instantly, every story she'd ever heard seemed to fall out of her head. She could remember nothing further than *Once upon a time*.

Pan tapped his fingers against the table.

"Once upon a time," Madge began.

He tilted his head.

"Uh…"

She struggled to latch onto something, anything, but her mind was blank. There was always a damsel in there somewhere, right? And a bad guy. And shoes. *Ugh.* She'd never been able to do anything under this kind of pressure.

He rolled his eyes. Clicked his tongue.

"Look," she said, "I can't think when you put me on the spot like that, so maybe you should just back off a little and give me some time to think."

Several of the boys gasped. The littlest one whimpered.

Pan's eyes narrowed, and the corners of his mouth turned up in a kind of sneer-smile. "You're right, girl. Besides, the best stories are the ones about me. You don't know any about me." He jumped up on the table and brandished his dagger. "Who wants to hear the story of how I cut off Captain Hook's hand?"

The boys whooped and smacked the table.

Madge paled. He'd cut off someone's hand? What was worse, he was bragging about it? Psycho.

Slightly extinguished half of the torches, leaving only those closest to Pan. Shadows danced over his face, making him appear ghoulish. The green of his eyes brightened against the darkness.

"It was a bright day with not a cloud in the sky. The clouds know to stay out of my way when I'm on a mission."

"Not this bleeding story again."

Madge frowned, studying the boys' faces for the source of the voice, but their attention was on Pan.

"The *Jolly Roger* was anchored just off the coast of Mermaid Lagoon. Captain James Hook stood at the bow, shooting Neverbirds for the fun of it."

"Cruel!" shouted one of the boys.

"Villain!" shouted another.

"Evil as Blackbeard!" Pan continued.

"Devil, he was!" Tootles added.

"That bloody well isn't true, and he knows it."

There was that voice again, the voice of a man, gravelly and low. Madge looked over her shoulder. The head of the pig, eyes popped out, sat atop a red-stained pike. Flies crept over the snout.

"Boy's delusional, in my opinion."

She froze. The voice sounded like it was coming from the pig. But that was impossible, wasn't it?

Pan's voice echoed in her mind: *nothing's impossible.*

"The skies are my domain." Pan lunged into the air and pointed down at Madge with fingers shaped like a gun. "With those pistol shots, Hook declared war on Neverland. On Peter Pan!"

"I don't have to listen to this bilge-sucking nonsense."

A faint gray light drifted from behind the pig head, followed closely behind by another, smaller light. Flares erupted from the sides of the lights that looked suspiciously like arms.

Parrying midair, Pan was absorbed in his tale. Curiosity pulled Madge in the direction of the lights. If she was careful, she could slip away without Pan noticing. There was no telling how long the story would last, but based on the boys' goading, it would be a while before it was over. She slid down in the chair until she was on all fours and then crawled toward the jungle path, illuminated by the wisps.

She moved quickly, fully expecting Pan to come swooping down and drag her back to the table and his terrible story. When, after several yards, he still hadn't come, she stood and followed the rapidly moving wisps on foot.

Madge finally caught up with them when they stopped to hover over a pond. Small yellow fish mouths poked through the surface, releasing rings of smoke into the air. She stooped behind a tree and watched the reflection of the larger wisp ripple across the water. She could barely make out a face with a long nose and prominent chin.

"You shouldn't let it bother ye, Captain," a voice said. It was different from the first, higher pitched and nasal.

"Aye, Smee. But the cretin mocks me even in death. No man deserves such a thing."

"A plague on anyone who dares to tarnish the good name of Captain James Hook."

"I'll drink to that!"

And then they both fell quiet, their glow dimming slightly.

Madge felt a strange mixture of fear and awe. She was pretty sure she was looking at the ghosts of Pan's pirates. Torn between squatting behind a bush like a voyeur and approaching them, she tottered on the balls of her feet, craning her neck to get a better look.

"This is not a zoo, lass. If ye want to stare, ye might want to find a better hiding place."

Crap.

"Eh, Cap'n?"

The ghost of the captain waved the other one off. "Come out, girl. I'll not be harming ye. Not that I could even if I wanted to."

Against her better judgment, Madge emerged from behind the tree and took three tentative steps toward the ghosts.

"I won't bite. Got no teeth."

The second ghost chuckled.

"Oh, do shut up, Smee."

"Here, maybe this will help." The captain's phantasmal form seemed to harden and become more defined. Facial features plumped out of the mist, followed by a neck and shoulders and a full body clothed in black. The final touch was a long, leathery trench coat with a high collar. He looked solid. Alive.

"Strictly speaking, I don't like to be doing this. Doesn't seem right without me hook." He held up his right arm, which was missing the hand.

Madge took another few steps forward. The captain did seem less threatening this way. His expression was soft, with the corners of his mouth lifted slightly. In his eyes, she didn't see any of the villainy Pan and the boys portrayed. Why would they lie?

"You got a name, lass?"

"Madge."

"Madge what?"

"Darling."

The second ghost flopped into solid form with an audible plop, his belly round and hanging over his belt. "Mary, mother o' God."

The captain shushed him. "It's a pleasure to make your acquaintance, Miss Darling. You may call me Hook."

The other man cleared his throat.

Hook sighed. "And this lump is my first mate, Smee."

"Thank ye, Cap'n."

Madge tried not to stare at the empty space where Hook's hand should have been. "Are you the one from his story?"

"Codswollop," said Smee.

"Aye. It's my name in the story, but it's not *me*."

"So he didn't cut off your hand?"

"Cut it off and fed it to the great sea beast that stalks the open waters outside the lagoon."

"Fekkin' killed us, he did!" Smee raised his fist in the air.

"Bad form, Smee. There's a lady present."

"Apologies."

Madge shook her head. "Why would he kill you? Because of the birds?"

Hook's face darkened. "For the fun of it."

"Thinks killin' pirates is a sport, he does."

"But he's just a boy." Even as she said it, she knew it wasn't true. Anyone who was just a boy didn't fly, didn't cut off the hands of full-grown men, didn't lure a girl with empty promises in the middle of the night to a land that should only have existed in fairy tales. And yet, as she conjured the image of Pan in her mind, she saw exactly that—just a boy.

Hook placed a finger to his lips. "Listen."

Barely breaking through the stillness of the jungle, Madge heard it. Footsteps. A lump lodged in her throat. He'd come looking for her. She didn't know why the thought bubbled up fear and anxiety, but standing in front of a pair of men who claimed to have been murdered by Pan did nothing to calm her nerves.

Smee whimpered.

Hook bowed. "Goodbye for now, Miss Darling. I dare say we shall meet again."

The men dissolved out of their corporeal forms and drifted on into the jungle as the footsteps pounded behind her. She turned, expecting to meet Pan's piercing gaze. Instead, she saw Slightly weave through the brush. The knot in her chest loosened.

"Come on, girl. Now. Before he notices."

Madge jogged next to him, falling twice over thick roots, until they emerged back through the gap in the trees that led to the table.

"...and thus ended the life of the devilish captain and his scurvy crew."

"Hooray for Pan!" the boys shouted and threw leaves over his head.

He wore a crown made of twisted twigs, dancing beneath their praises. He turned and met Madge's eyes. He didn't seem to have noticed that she'd gone, or cared for that matter. "Well, girl? Was that not the best story ever told?"

Slightly kicked her heel.

She nodded enthusiastically. "Oh, yes. I loved it."

"Of course you did." Pan removed the crown then, thinking better of it, placed it back on his head. "I think that's enough excitement for one evening, gents. The Darling girl needs sleep."

The hairs on the back of her neck stood on end. She wondered if it was merely an aftereffect of having an interaction with ghosts or if her body sensed something her mind didn't. She wouldn't be sleeping tonight.

Like the rusted gears of an ancient clock, the wheels in Captain Hook's mind began to turn, slowly at first. Then as they gained momentum, a clear picture of what was to be done presented itself.

He smiled.

Smee settled next to the captain on the bank of a river avoided by Pan and his lot. There was a rumor that the waters of this river were tied to another realm. If not for want of a boat, the captain might have tried to sail there—wherever *there* was. But there was the little matter of his revenge. What kind of pirate captain would he be if he hadn't gotten his due before shipping off to uncharted waters? Before now, he had all but given up on the idea. What could a mere ghost, a being without true form, do? But with the Darling girl here... She could be useful.

"Glad to see your spirits lifting, Cap'n," Smee said. "Seems the girl put the color back in your whispies."

"Indeed."

A sharp-toothed koi pounced on one of the smaller goldfish, obliterating the thing with one gnash of its teeth. Smee collapsed in a fit of giggles. Of all the people Hook had imagined spending the afterlife with, his first mate was leagues away from the top of the list. The dolt only served as a reminder of all he'd lost at the hands of that boy.

Smee wheezed. "D'ya see that, Cap'n? The Kraken rises again!"

Still, Smee was good for a laugh.

"Ready the cannons!" Hook thrust a make-believe sword into the air. "I'll have the beast's face for a figurehead!"

Chapter Thirteen

I T WAS LIKE THE TREE house saw into Pan's mind. Madge went inside first, squinting against the brightness of the lamps hanging from vines. Pan followed shortly after. As he crossed the threshold, the lamps dimmed, and the braided branches above them separated to allow slivers of the night sky to be visible. The full moon shined a spotlight on Pan, tracking his every step.

At a gesture of Pan's hand, the boys scrambled into their prospective bunks carved into the walls of the main room. Slightly lingered behind a moment and then left Madge alone with Pan. Even with Pan standing uncomfortably close to her, scrutinizing her—always scrutinizing—with those eyes, the warmth of the tree house and watchful gaze of the stars had a calming effect on Madge. Fatigue kneaded her muscles. But she was disappointed in herself. An entire day had passed—how did that happen?—and she was no closer to finding her mother. Somehow, she felt further away than ever.

"You lied to me," she said.

"When?"

"My mother. You promised—"

Pan rolled his eyes. "You're going to have to learn to trust me first."

"And if I don't?"

"Your loss, I guess." He pointed to a bunk. Her backpack was in it. "Bed."

She scoffed. "You're giving me orders now?"

"I give orders. You take them. That's how things work here. Right, boys?"

Fatigued voices murmured, "Aye."

That was it. First chance she got, Madge was out of here.

She turned her back on Pan and climbed into her bunk. When he fell asleep, she'd make her move. After all those nights at Grandma Wendy's, she was a pro.

The bunk wasn't so small that Madge couldn't lie down, but it was almost impossible to lie any other way but on her back. The bed of leaves stabbed at her neck and the soft part behind her knees. She used her backpack as a pillow. It helped a little. Unable to fold her arms over her stomach comfortably, they stayed flat at her sides. The way the bunk curled up at her sides and the top of her head made it feel like a coffin.

Her fingers traced the wood. Smooth. Then she felt a dip in the surface. She recognized the loop and line of writing. Someone had carved something in the side. Madge sat up and pulled down one of the lanterns hanging above her. It barely gave, but it was just enough to cast light over the carving: Wendy Darling. And below that, Jane Darling.

Trust me, Pan had said.

She traced the grooves of her mother's name over and over until her fingertips were raw. Her mother had been here, had maybe slept in this bunk. So where was she now? Madge felt up the sides of the bunk, searching for another sign of her mother's presence, but only managed to get a splinter. For now, though, she had a name carved in a bunk. It was enough for Madge to decide to stay.

They went way back, Pan and Slightly. In fact, it felt to Slightly that there had never been a time in which he hadn't been second in command to the leader of the Lost Boys, Pan's confidant. Slightly's was the voice of reason—or as much reason as Pan permitted. And occasionally, Slightly was Pan's personal thing-holder.

He sat at Pan's feet, holding the base of a log. It was thick and gnarled and reminded him of the time Nibs broke his arm. The bone had poked through and never set properly. Nibs called it his magic arm. Wood shavings rained down on Slightly's head, sticking to his hair and eyelashes as Pan whittled away above him, using only the stars to see by. Slightly wanted to bring the log back to the tree house, but Peter insisted on carving it where they'd found it.

"What do you think she'd like more?" Pan said. "A bust of me or a full body?"

Though Slightly would admit that his leader possessed many talents, woodwork was not one of them. Loathe to reveal his weakness to the men, Pan preferred to prune *them* to fit the beds they slept in. Flesh was easy to manipulate. Wood wasn't.

Slightly, however, was an excellent carver. Before Pan had discovered and destroyed them, Slightly had kept a collection of his creations, mostly figures of small animals. While he wouldn't cross Pan again for one of the other boys, he suspected he would have for Madge had she not fit in Wendy's old bed.

Pan was not the type to please someone other than himself. It didn't make sense for him to want to work at something he was terrible at just to give Madge a gift, even if she was Wendy's granddaughter. Slightly could speculate all he wanted in his head, but asking questions would likely get his head cut off. "I think she would be happy with either one."

"Yes." Pan paused to admire his work in progress. "She would. And yet…"

Slightly tensed.

"She's different, don't you think?"

"Different how?"

"Don't be stupid. You know what I mean."

"She is a little… strange," Slightly conceded. And pretty. Prettier than the Wendy lady. Prettier even than Jane, with her soft white skin and deep brown eyes. He shook away these dangerous thoughts.

"Strange. Yes." Pan's voice trailed off. He focused on his work, and shavings flew. "I might keep her."

"And if she wants to leave?"

"Why would anyone want to leave Neverland?" Pan laughed. "You know, sometimes I wonder if you're dumber than the great meat-for-brains, Tootles."

Slightly kept his eyes trained on an ant crawling between slits in the floor. "Wendy wanted to leave."

Pan paused, rock raised over the chisel. Slightly saw out of the corner of his eye that Pan held his breath. The subject of Wendy was a dangerous one, but for some reason, Slightly needed to know Pan's mind regarding Madge.

"Wendy was weak," Pan said finally. "It takes a special girl to handle the Spring Cleaning."

"And you think Madge is special?"

"You doubt me?"

"No. She is special."

"I'm glad you agree because as of this moment, I make it your duty to protect her."

Slightly hesitated. "Have... have I done something to upset you?"

Pan grinned, all teeth. "Why, whatever do you mean, Lieutenant?"

Pan knew exactly what Slightly meant. It was no coincidence that when one of Pan's girls died or disappeared, her appointed protector followed her to her fate. Pan wanted Slightly dead. The only question was why.

Chapter Fourteen

PAN TURNED THE PAGES OF Wendy's diary with mounting fury. She used a lot of big words, but he could read enough to understand. He'd always known she was trouble, but it wasn't until now that he realized what she truly was: a traitor.

Plotting against him the entire time, it seemed. Oh, how he hated her.

Madge was finally asleep. Pan watched her chest rising and falling from his chair and tried in vain to see into her mind. Was she a miniature Wendy? Only time would tell. Slightly liked her in that disgusting way adults liked each other. It was stupidly obvious, the way he got all pink in the cheeks when Madge was in earshot, how he went out of the way to make her feel comfortable. There was a stab of jealousy as Pan thought of how Slightly looked at her. Madge belonged to Pan, not him.

A thought occurred to Pan, and he grinned. Slightly's puppy love was a sure sign that he was growing up, which was against the law. He'd need to be dealt with.

Pan restlessly paced the length of the main room. Even with the Slightly issue to look forward to, Pan was bored. There hadn't been any pirates to fight since Hook—that was ages ago—and the Red Men had gotten smart. Their camp moved frequently and unexpectedly and was almost impossible to track. It drove Pan mad. This was *his* island! How were they able to hide from him?

But boredom wasn't the only thing on Pan's mind tonight. Something was happening to Neverland. It was growing wild and harder to control. The day and night still obeyed him, but spring came and went without his permission. Neverbirds no longer came when he called. Most of the big game had disappeared. The pig for Madge's feast was the first in forever. It was only a matter of time before Pan's enemies noticed and took action the way he had that day on Hook's ship. He couldn't let that happen.

He'd need fresh blood, new Lost Boys to give the island the youth it needed—he needed—to survive. But without a ship, he could only transport a few at a time, and pixie dust was becoming scarce. The mermaids were stalling. They wanted something from him. Pan made a note to net a few of their children to trade.

Madge let out a sigh. She must have been dreaming.   Pan didn't dream anymore. All he saw when he closed his eyes was a wash of red. All he felt was cold.

It didn't always used to be that way. At least, he didn't think so. He couldn't remember.

Disgusted with Wendy's ramblings, he slammed the diary closed and stuffed it back into the bag. He'd been planning to just kill Madge, but now, he decided, he'd keep her, turn her into the very thing Wendy dreaded.

While his Lost Boys slept, Pan flew into the night to tell the stars his plan.

Madge jolted awake, bolting upright and smacking her forehead against a lantern. A dirty hand that smelled like human feces clamped over her mouth. In the near darkness, she could barely make out a wide shadow and a pair of golden eyes. At first, she thought it was one of the Lost Boys and tried to pry off the hand, but the grip was too strong to belong to a kid. Another pair of hands tied her wrists together and covered her eyes with a moldy cloth.

Madge tried to scream. Fingers pinched her windpipe, cutting off the sound.

Quick and silent as a fox, the intruder tossed her over his shoulder and whisked her out of the tree house into the unknown jungle.

Slightly didn't have to open his eyes to know that Pan hovered over him. Fury radiated from Pan in almost audible waves. Slightly took a brief second to gather his thoughts then opened his eyes.

Pan's face glowed like smoldering coals threatening to burst into flame. All it needed was something to devour. Slightly didn't dare ask what was wrong; Pan's left hand trembled over the hilt of his dagger.

"Do you smell it?"

At the moment, the only thing Slightly smelled was Pan's rich, hot breath. He turned his head. The stench was faint, but there: shit and saffron and oil. "Red Men," he whispered.

"You had one duty."

Slightly scrambled to sit up. "No."

"She's gone."

"Maybe she's just gone out to take a piss," he said pitifully. "Or *wash*. You know girls and their habits."

"If we don't find her—"

"We will."

Pan held up his hand, fingers spread. Five fingers. Five days: the longest anyone new to Neverland had survived in the jungle alone. Five days until, if Madge wasn't returned safely to the tree house, Slightly faced the sword.

Madge's captor ran beneath her. Her stomach bounced against his pointed shoulder. The motion made her sick and dizzy. The rush of his breath through his nose, crickets playing their ironic symphony, nocturnal birds alerting each other to the intrusion—these were the sounds she heard, along with the disturbing absence of footsteps crunching over the jungle floor.

They stuffed another of those moldy cloths in her mouth. Tears and snot streamed down her face, and she struggled not to gag on her own mucus. Her captor stopped suddenly and dropped her on the ground. The cloth around her eyes fell away, and something sharp sliced through her arm, sending white-hot pain up through her shoulder.

"You walk," someone said.

They yanked her up by the elbow. Something popped, and her breath caught. She spit out the putrid cloth. "Where are you taking me?"

A slap. She saw stars. Her cheek throbbed.

"No talk. Walk."

He stabbed her shoulder with a finger, propelling her forward.

The sun started to rise, but the light of dawn did little to help her navigate the fallen branches, vines, and skittering rodents that tried to trip her. Those first few rays, though, were enough to show Madge her captor.

He was built like a tree—solid trunk with long, branch-like limbs. His black hair was tied tightly at the back of his head, revealing scars running from his temple, down the side of his neck, and ending in thick lines on his bare shoulders. Dried red paint covered his chest and face in splashes. His expression was unreadable.

They walked in silence for a long time. Occasionally, the painted man shoved her in a new direction. It felt like they were walking in circles. The jungle backdrop became frustratingly familiar with each passing moment. After a while, Madge noticed that they weren't alone. Leaping from tree to tree above them was another painted man. He was smaller, wearing some kind of poncho that looked like wings. A giant red bird of prey. Flanking them on either side were more painted men. They moved delicately through the brush, not at all like Madge's pathetic stumbling. If she thought she had any chance to run, it disappeared in an instant.

Like separate limbs of the same animal, all of the painted men stopped simultaneously. The one escorting her sniffed the air.

"You wait," he said without looking at her. But as though to reiterate the futility of her escape, he withdrew a sharpened stone weapon from the wrap covering the lower half of his body.

She hugged herself against a sudden chilly breeze while the painted man inched forward, disappearing behind a cluster of dried palm fronds. The men above her whistled, each sound as unique as a birdcall. A faint plume of smoke rose from behind the brush, and the men converged on her like a wave, eyeing her hungrily. Madge shuddered, positive they were going to kill her, maybe even eat her—roast her on a spit like Pan's pig.

And where the hell was Pan? The boys? Were they even awake? Had they noticed that she was missing? Was this another one of his games?

The painted men stood in a half circle around her and pushed her forward, their hands like paddles against her back and ass. They herded her—a cow on the ramp to the slaughterhouse.

"Stop!" She dug her heels into the ground, but the force of the men shoved her forward.

The smoke turned orange then red and smelled like charred skin. How many others had these painted people devoured?

A sad, steady drumbeat echoed around her, and at first, she thought it was the sound of her own heart. Tears obscured the smoke and jungle until they were a coppery blur. A pair of hands engulfed her shoulders and directed her past the palm fronds. Smoke burned her nose and throat, and she hacked dryly. Her tongue itched, and her chest was knotted. She rubbed her eyes to clear the water and smoke. The men continued to push her until she could feel the smoke caress her skin.

Madge blinked away a few remaining tears and saw the first painted man. He stood next to a mound of glowing coals. Behind him, a woman with black hair so long it dragged on the ground and painted skin like the man held a stone knife against his chest. She scraped roughly, and swatches of red peeled away before landing on the coals. His chest was now pink and smooth. Scarred.

Not paint. Skin.

"Come," the woman said.

Madge couldn't help thinking she'd seen these people on late-night television at some point, all tomahawks and beads and windswept hair. *They're going to scalp me*, she thought. Her head tingled.

"Do not be afraid."

Easy for you to say. She swallowed. "That's kind of impossible with you holding a knife like that."

The woman seemed to just notice the weapon in her hands. She smiled and wrapped it in a strip of cloth then stored it beneath a pile of leaves. "Better?"

Madge stole a glance over her shoulder. The men were gone. Silent. Instant. Creepy.

"Come."

Faced with no other option, Madge approached the woman, allowing her to take Madge's hand. The woman's palm was rough with calluses but gentle. Up close, it was impossible to be sure of the woman's age. Lines cut her face and skin. Where the redness bled into a lighter, pinker color, her skin was freckled and dimpled, but there was a spark in her golden eyes. They were lively and inquisitive. Youthful.

The woman led Madge into a clearing where a collection of huts made from leaves and light branches surrounded a pit. The huts were draped with cloth to give the illusion of privacy, but against the sunlight, Madge made out the shadows of their inhabitants. The face of a child, no older than five or six, peered out from behind a flap of cloth, his eyes wide as plates. She smiled at him. He stuck out his tongue but kept his eyes firmly locked on her until an arm snatched him back inside.

The woman pulled Madge into one of the smaller huts. Inside, it smelled of dirt and cheap medicinal lotion like the kind Grandma Wendy used. A brown blanket was spread out in the corner. Opposite that was a display of pots and bowls, some filled, others empty. A bundle of twigs lay next to it, about the size of Madge's forearm, wrapped with a purple vine. One end was charred.

"Off," the woman said.

"What?"

"Off." The woman pantomimed stripping off her poncho.

Madge gripped the hem of her shirt. "No way."

The woman clicked her tongue. Madge wasn't prepared for the woman's strength. With a few rough tugs she had Madge stripped to her underwear and bra. When the woman tried to make a grab for those, Madge smacked her arm. The woman brushed it off like a mosquito bite.

"You stink," she said. "I clean."

Madge frowned. "Well, you smell like twice-baked crap."

Again, the woman waved her indifference and then dipped her hands into the largest pot. As she withdrew them, clear oil dripped from her fingertips.

"Clean."

Madge stepped back. "No."

The woman grunted and seized Madge by her wrist. The smell of the oil was sharp but not wholly unpleasant as the woman worked it over

Madge's skin and through her hair. Though it dried almost instantly on her skin, it seemed to magically remove the grit of the previous day, leaving her feeling like she'd just had a shower.

Madge pried herself out of the woman's grasp and tried to get at her clothes.

The woman nudged Madge away with her wide hips. "Dirty."

"But that's all I have! What am I supposed to wear?"

From a box Madge hadn't noticed before, the woman pulled out a length of dark-green cloth. Carrying Madge's clothes, she left Madge to figure out a way to dress herself.

Madge wrapped the cloth around her middle, then slung the remaining bit over her shoulder and tucked the excess into the back. All the important bits were covered, but it was uncomfortable, and she didn't know if she'd be able to walk two steps without having it fall off. She dug around in the box for something she could use as a belt. Her best option ended up being a strip of unforgiving leather that took several knots to remain tied around her waist.

"Call me Jungle Jane," she muttered.

"Is that your name?" a voice said.

Madge yipped and spun to face the intruder. He was old and shriveled but stood with a straight back—a man who knew his age but commanded the respect that came with the distinction. His skin was covered in more red patches than the others, and he wore a band of woven feathers around his head. A long silver braid fell over his shoulder.

"I'm sorry to frighten you," he said through a mischievous grin. "Once a man learns to tread lightly, it is hard to break the habit."

"Yeah. Okay. Whatever."

"Forgiveness freely given is a treasure. Thank you."

Madge raised an eyebrow. "Sure."

"Now, as to my first question—I know that you are not Jane. She was taller than you, though there is a bit of a resemblance."

Adrenaline pulsed behind her eyes. "You knew my—"

The man put up his hand. "All in good time. May I have *your* name, please?"

"You first."

He nodded knowingly. "I, too, know the power of giving another being your name. Our names are like our souls, are they not?"

Madge shifted her weight and crossed her arms.

"I am called Elder."

"Madge."

He closed his eyes and whispered her name, as though trying it out on his mouth. "Beautiful name. It suits you."

"Can we move past the pleasantries and get to why you kidnapped me?"

"As I said, all in good time. But don't worry, dear Madge. We won't hurt you."

"Who is 'we'?"

A veil of sadness drifted over his features. "The Red Men."

"All of you?"

He nodded.

"They don't talk like you. It's like they don't understand me. Why?"

"They pretend not to."

She paused. "Why?"

"Because it is part of their story. They refuse to relinquish it."

"Story?"

He smiled and tilted his head.

Madge sighed. "Yeah, all in good time, whatever."

"Come. I will show you the village."

From the diary of Wendy Moira Angela Darling

Wicked tramp.

Harlot.

Devil.

Oh, the names I wish I would allow to pass my lips. None come close enough to describing that despicable red princess, Tiger Lily. She thinks I wouldn't notice the way she dances for him, the way she smiles from beneath long, fluttering eyelashes. Peter, of course, cannot be blamed. What boy wouldn't be turned by a blatant taunt?

For the first time since coming to Neverland, I wish I could talk to my mother. She would know what to do. I'd need both hands to count the number of times Father has strayed, only to be pulled back by Mother's beauty and charm. I fear my body may forever be that of a young lady, but my mind and heart will grow into a woman. A woman who is in love with a boy. Was there ever a story more tragic?

He loves the princess. I can see it on his face as plain as day. Stupid. Her hair is like Nana's after rolling in mud, and her lips are thin and twisted. She's a savage. Probably doesn't even wash regularly.

But they all love her. John fought Slightly for the pleasure of passing her a bowl of putrid broth, earning a broken nose for his trouble. Even Michael (my heart!) crawled into her lap as she told a boring story about the wind and its torrid love affair with the mountain. He gave her the yellow ribbon I'd tied around his wrist as a thank-you gift. MY ribbon.

What I did later, Diary, was necessary. It was vital to our relationship. I will accept all responsibility in the future as long as it leads to Peter's eyes and longings returning to me.

I killed a Neverbird, Peter's favorite, with the long white feathers and blue-green eyes as deep and clear as the ocean. And then I planted a dirty yellow feather, plucked from Tiger Lily's pet, in the gash.

I thought I saw one of the boys running away as I arranged the bird to look as ugly as possible. I can't be sure who it was, but Slightly won't look at me. It doesn't matter. If it came down to it, Peter would take my word over Slightly's. I'm sure of it.

When I returned to the fire, not even the princess's blatant flirtations could bother me. She may be the daughter of a chief, but I am a Darling. Perhaps it's the shock of having committed murder still coursing through my veins, but as I stood over the bird and demanded Peter love only me, it seemed as though Neverland itself heard—and heeded—my call.

Chapter Fifteen

Once upon a time...

DYING WASN'T AT ALL WHAT Hook imagined it would be. No white light. No boatman. No escort to Davey Jones's Locker. Only pain and cold.

Of course, he hadn't imagined dying by the hand of a child, either, but the fates were cruel and not to be taunted. He supposed he should've been thankful. Conventional faith would've put him in the fiery pits of Hell after his last breath shuddered from his body. Instead, he'd woken up—pain gone, but the cold remained—as a specter, still trapped on that God-forsaken island.

In a way, it *was* Hell. He didn't have to see the carnage to know his entire crew had been slaughtered, taken in the dead of night with little chance of defending themselves. The villains cut Smee's throat while he slept.

Devils.

Smee, more than any of those bilge rats, deserved to cross into someplace better, but the man was loyal to a fault and stayed behind with his captain. It was an act Hook would not soon forget.

With nothing to look forward to but life eternal, Hook's sole purpose became revenge—revenge on Pan, his boys, on the whole bloody island. He'd have burned it to the ground if he could, but without proper form, Hook was grossly limited.

Before he'd died, Hook had noticed that Pan was rather taken with a certain young lady he'd brought to the island—maybe not taken so much as intrigued, as a shark is intrigued by a wounded seal. He decided that she could be the key to Pan's undoing.

The first time Hook came to Wendy, she refused to acknowledge him, loyal to Pan or to her sanity. The second, she cursed him. The third, she listened.

He'd found the girl wandering the forest outside the Red Man camp. Tears stained her pale face, and cold fury burned in her eyes. Her nightgown was tattered and stained at the bottom with mud and something else. She didn't wear shoes. Her hair was pulled back by a piece of twine; escaped curls framed her face. She muttered. Kicked the long grass. Threw rocks.

Hook approached carefully, keeping his distance. An angry woman was like a doe. One must be calm. Cautious. "Is there something the matter, my lady?"

Wendy sneered. "As if it's any of your business, pirate."

"You're right. It's not. But pirate or no, a man can't abide a young woman in trouble." Still getting used to his new form, Hook struggled to reach a seated position on a fallen log. "Is there something I can do?"

"Can you kill a red princess?" Wendy's eyes widened at her own question. She slapped her hands over her mouth.

"Alas, I cannot." He wriggled his ghostly fingers. "I'm nothing but a shadow now."

She sat next to Hook, head bowed. "I shouldn't have said that."

"Ah, but words are only that, my lady."

"Not if you mean them," she whispered.

He nodded sagely. The girl wouldn't need much pushing. "*Especially* if you mean them. For what are words without meaning but the inane ramblings of a mind come undone?"

"I fear precisely that."

"Love does eat away at the mind." Hook placed a hand on her leg. It passed right through. Her trembling lip set into a thin line, and her eyes widened in badly disguised surprise. "Oh, don't look at me like that. Anyone can see the way you feel about the boy."

Her expression fell. "It's that obvious?"

"Aye."

"Not to him."

"He's a cretin."

Wendy nodded sadly. "He loves that savage princess, Tiger Lily."

"It is a convenient love affair."

"What does that mean?"

Hook paused, waited for her eyes to grow wide with hope. "Peter Pan will never admit it, but he needs the Red Men. Their power. Because though he may control the island, it is balanced by the savages. Should they decide to take the island, they could. This peace treaty"—he spat the words—"is nothing but a necessary evil. We both know what Pan wants, what he really wants, is to wipe them out completely, to hold Neverland's power for his own."

She sniffed. "Why doesn't he, then?"

"Because Peter Pan fancies himself a kind of hero. He won't make a move without reason."

She bit her lip. "It wouldn't have to be a very good reason, would it?"

Wendy was a smart girl.

Hook held up his handless arm. "No. It wouldn't."

A pair of Neverbirds flew in a circle overhead before landing on a branch. The larger one pecked at a notch in the trunk while the smaller ruffled its feathers.

"Pan loves those things," Wendy said. "I think they're ugly."

"It's not what they are. It's what they represent."

"Which is?"

"He sees them as an extension of himself. A threat to the birds is a threat to Peter Pan. Though it's no secret he sees you in them as well. Is it true you were once mistaken for a Neverbird?"

Wendy nodded, gaze fixed on the birds.

Hook grinned. "I'd better be on my way, Miss Darling. It was a pleasure talking with you tonight."

She didn't speak, and her small, girlish hands dug into the bark of the log. Her eyes, bright with purpose, followed the Neverbirds' every twitch.

Chapter Sixteen

T HEY LOOKED EVERYWHERE, BUT MADGE was gone. With each snarl from Pan's lips, Slightly felt sicker. It wasn't the fact that his life hung in the balance that turned his stomach, though. It was that there was no question of the culprit. Their sulfuric, sweet-rancid smell was like a calling card. The rogue Red Men. And Pan would want to go directly to their chief, Tiger Lily.

Once upon a time, the Red Men and the Lost Boys had been on decent terms. Slightly had even taken a few hunting lessons from their best warriors. Then Pan decided the Red Men had somehow broken the treaty. Something about birds. The then chief, Tiger Lily's father, was killed. The war. A splitting of the tribe. Now, the Lost Boys didn't venture into Red Men territory unless Pan led the expedition. Even then, there was a significant chance of being scalped or gutted.

"Arm yourselves," Pan said.

The boys pulled their favorite weapons from their bunks, slinging bows over shoulders and stuffing knives into their pockets. Slightly absently stroked the expert stitching along one of his shirt pockets. Wendy had been telling them the story of a girl with golden hair trapped in a tower when she'd sewn this. *Do girls always need rescuing?* he'd asked. The memory made him sad but also determined. He would rescue Madge. He would be the knight in shining armor. Slightly carried a spear in one hand; in the other, he cradled a pocketknife. The handle was smooth, polished wood, and the blade gleamed from repeated cleanings. He'd had it for as long as he could remember, but where it came from was a mystery. The only clue was an inscription. Nibs had to read it to Slightly back when Nibs still remembered how to read. *Edward, 1884.* It was only a knife, and a little one at that, but for some reason, it made Slightly feel good to carry it, centered, like it was the glue that kept the pieces of his self together.

They set out for the Yellow-Tree Hills, a small area of Neverland where the Red Men were known to make camp during the warm months. Pan, as usual, took the lead, but Slightly hung at the back of the group instead of at Pan's side. He told himself that it was for the protection of the group. Someone needed to watch their backs. It wasn't entirely untrue.

Of all the times Slightly had come up against the Red Men, he'd never left the battle with fewer than three near-fatal wounds. Capable warriors with more at stake than a stupid game, the Red Men fought for their very survival, which made them dangerous. There was a real chance of dying, which scared Slightly more than it used to.

The new kids? They didn't remember a time before Peter. Slightly had been there when it all came crashing down on Hook's ship. He'd watched the blood seep into the deck. Slightly hadn't even blinked because, at the time, it felt right. The pirates took, Pan gave, and the boys suffered for it. They'd lived on tree bark, bitter leaves, and resentment. As soon as Pan delivered their only catch—a couple of gangly rabbits—to the pirates, the Lost Boys, Slightly included, had been done.

Then Peter took the sword, and by that, the right to rule Neverland, and the boys fell in line like good little soldiers. Slightly had followed.

Now? Now he wondered how long before Peter looked at Slightly the way Pan looked at Peter. With fear. Suspicion. The difference, of course, was that Peter would always be the one to strike first.

The inhabitants of the village emerged slowly, poking their noses from between huts and trees like frightened mice. The sight of Elder, though, seemed to instill a kind of trust in them. Madge wasn't a threat.

"You see the children? Grandmothers and grandfathers?"

Madge grunted acknowledgement.

"Unlike Pan and his boys, we are native to this island. We are part of its rhythm. We grow. We live. We die. Slower, yes, since the first Pan was brought here by the fairies, but still we grow. Pan claims this is a weakness, but he is a boy. Boys only know to the ends of their noses."

The ground had been cleared of twigs and jungle debris, revealing the red clay beneath, which created narrow paths through the camp. Between each hut, modest gardens were cordoned off by fences made from thick, ropy vines and what looked like bones. She recognized the little red sweet tomatoes from Pan's feast.

Elder tried to hold her hand, but she snatched it away.

"How long have you been on the island, dear?" he asked.

"Don't know. When I left, it was night, and when we got here, it was day. I lay down, and it was night, and now..." She gestured to the rising sun.

He nodded. "It is impossible to track the days with the sun. It, too, obeys the Pan."

"It's the sun," she said, incredulous. "No one controls the sun."

"By now he will have noticed you are missing. He is a good hunter. It is easier to search in the light."

He directed her toward a rock wall, partially obscured by thick vines and orange blossoms. "I want to show you something."

"No, thanks."

"You don't trust me?"

"You kidnapped me. Pretty sure you've got to keep me locked in a basement for a while with nothing but a photo of you and a can of tuna before Stockholm Syndrome kicks in."

Elder frowned. "Are you ill?"

"No. I'm not ill." She sighed. "And I don't trust you."

"We *saved* you."

"From what? Spiders? Scurvy?"

Elder's expression lifted. "Please. Come."

"Fine. But you're in front where I can see you."

"Fair enough."

Elder lifted the bottom of his robe as he crossed through the brush. Madge followed, wondering if he had some kind of weapon in the folds. He was old but probably fast. She'd have been better off making a run for it. If what he said was right, that Pan brought the sun to suit his needs, he was out there looking for her right now. All she'd have to do was scream.

The brush thinned until it parted into a clearing. Tree limbs hung dry and cracking over a dozen or more boulders the size of car tires sanding sentry behind mounds of dirt. White flower petals dusted the smooth surfaces.

"A cemetery," Madge said.

Elder nodded. "The only one of its kind in Neverland. The Red Men go to their next lives atop a fire of willow branches. The Lost Boys... can't be bothered to bury their dead. There are some, though, that, for them, neither option is appropriate."

"Like who?"

"Look around."

Cemeteries gave Madge the creeps—one too many zombie movie marathons. She kept herself out of grabbing distance as she trudged down the first aisle. At first, the names and picture epigraphs meant nothing to her. *Jared Snow* above a hand with an eye at the center. *Edward Evans* surrounded by a wreath of ivy. *Ivan Luknavitch* beneath a clover. Then toward the back, a name on one of the largest stones caught her eye.

Johnathan Darling beneath a top hat.

Grandma Wendy's brother, John?

"Is that..."

"Keep looking," Elder said.

It felt like someone was breathing on the back of her neck. She couldn't stop scratching it, but the feeling only got worse.

The next two stones bore the names Abigail Darling and Nathan Darling. Madge had never met her cousins, but she knew of them. Grandma Wendy had spoken about them like characters out of a fairy tale. Otherworldly. Perfect. Madge hated them.

Another stone stood out. Its edges were coated in a reddish tinge, like it'd been rubbed with clay.

"We sacrifice our skin to the fire so that it will shield us. Shield them." Elder frowned. "It does not always help."

Part of her didn't want to look. Her body tingled and then went numb. Her ears rang, and her teeth clenched. She didn't blink. Somehow, her feet propelled her forward until she stood directly in front of the stone, toes grazing the mound of dirt. Beneath a carving of a wilted rose was the name.

Jane Darling.

"No." Madge felt paralyzed. A bit of dirt slipped from the mound. It landed on her shoe, and she gasped.

"Jane was special. She was kind to us."

Madge shook her head. "No. It's... no."

She wouldn't believe it. She knew her mother was alive. In Chicago. Waiting for her.

"It was the least we could do. Such a grim fate. Such a bright-hearted soul. I believe that if it weren't for Pan, she wouldn't have done it."

"Done what?"

"She wouldn't have taken her own life."

Madge's knees buckled, and her eyes burned. Elder held her up by her shoulders. Bile burned her throat, the world spun, and she couldn't make sense of what was in front of her face. Pan had promised to take her to her mother. Was this what he'd meant?

Elder continued, "The fairies abandoned him soon after. They loved Jane. We all did."

"You're lying," Madge said. "You have to be."

"I understand, dear. I—"

"No!" Madge tore his arms away from her. Tears spilled down her face. Her nose ran, and her ears popped when she tried to breathe. "My mother is alive. She has to be."

"Because you want her to be."

"Because I need her!" Madge covered her face, tried to wipe the image of her mother's grave from her memory. "Because she can't be dead. Because if she's dead, Grandma Wendy was right. She *left* me."

Elder's arms closed tight around her shaking body. It hurt, but she didn't shove him away this time. He guided her hand to the stone and forced her to keep it there. To feel it. To know it. To accept—

"I can't," she whispered.

"She didn't leave you."

"Then why is she here?"

Elder offered a sad smile. "Why are you here?"

Madge wiped her face and thought of Pan, appearing when she was scared, offering her exactly what she wanted in a moment when she would have done anything to get it. Had he offered her mother something? What?

A gentle caw broke the fragile silence. Above them, a great bird with red and orange feathers and a neck like a swan circled. She'd only ever seen drawings of phoenixes in fantasy books. Part of her yearned to touch it.

Elder nodded to the bird, which flapped its long wings and climbed into the sky. "She is ready to see you."

"Who?"

"Chief Tiger Lily."

Madge worried that if she left the cemetery, she would forget, and then Elder would have to bring her back, and the grief would destroy her all over again. She couldn't take her eyes from her mother's name, carved deeply into the stone. She traced the outline as though memorizing the roughness with her skin.

"Come."

Madge allowed him to lead her out of the clearing but glanced back with each step, worried that if she looked away for too long, it'd disappear.

Tiger Lily's hut was no larger than the others, but feathers and polished stones adorned the door flap. A single orange lily grew from a small patch of green and turned its face up at Madge as she approached.

Elder touched the delicate petals. "She is young, but she is brave. She will make a great leader one day."

A voice came from inside. "One day, Elder?"

He smiled. With one hand on her back, he escorted Madge beneath the flap. The chief sat cross-legged in the center of a red mat. Other than a staff tied with string and animal skin, there was no other decoration. Weapons lay neatly on the ground beside her. They resembled the chief herself, all sharp edges. Her golden eyes were little more than slits, and her lips were set in a tight line. Her hair was braided, trailing from the top of her head to a coiled pile beside her like the charred snake on Pan's table. Only the bottom half of her body was covered. Her breasts—small, brown mounds—rose and fell with her breath.

Elder bowed his head slightly. "The ramblings of an old man are meant to be ignored."

The flicker of a smile touched Tiger Lily's mouth. "Old man, yours are the only ramblings not to be ignored." Her gaze fell on Madge. "This is the girl, then?"

He nodded.

"Leave us."

He retrieved a bowl and skin sack from somewhere in his robe. "Forgive me, but tradition must be observed."

Tiger Lily closed her eyes, *probably to roll them*, Madge thought, and held out her hand. Elder poured a small amount of green liquid in two bowls before placing one of them in her hand. They sipped in silence. Madge became painfully aware of her hands dangling uncomfortably at her sides. Finished, Elder collected his items, stowing them back in his robe. He flashed one last smile at Madge before exiting.

Tiger Lily waited a beat and then turned her head and spit the liquid into the dirt. Scraping her tongue with her nails, she gagged and shuddered. She smacked her tongue a few times before fixing her gaze on Madge. "Sorry. Nasty stuff."

"What is it?"

"I don't know, honestly, and don't care to find out. My father drank it with the elders at each meeting, as did his father before him. A long tradition of drinking sludge that tastes of urine and sour root when saying goodbye works just as well and doesn't leave you squatting over a hole for hours at a time. Better to just spit it out when no one's looking."

"Gross."

"Indeed." Tiger Lily stood and approached Madge. Her braid dragged behind her like a tail. "You look old."

Madge frowned. "I'm fourteen."

Tiger Lily knelt, ignoring her, and sniffed uncomfortably close to Madge's crotch.

Madge skittered backward, hunched over. "What the hell?"

"Have you bled?"

Sneering, Madge shoved the chief's shoulder. She might as well have tried to shove a mountain. Tiger Lily nodded, as though that explained everything. When she stood, she was only an inch or two taller than Madge, but her muscles were firm and her shoulders square. Strong. Intimidating. Madge inched backward.

"I can smell him on you."

"Who?"

"Who do you think?"

Madge remembered the way Pan kissed her face, and her cheeks burned. "All I smell is that green crap."

Tiger Lily laughed ruefully. "It's hard to believe you're a Darling. The others weren't nearly as spirited." She frowned. "But then, I didn't get to them until after..."

"After what?"

She brushed Madge's question away like a bug. "It's fortunate because spirit is exactly what I'm looking for."

"In what?"

"You're going to do something for me." Tiger Lily lifted the corner of her rug and retrieved a small trinket.

She handed it to Madge, who turned it over in her palm. A ring. The band was tarnished silver, but the round opal at the center shone. There was an inscription on the inside of the band, barely legible, but the J was unmistakable.

"My mother's ring?" Madge stroked the stone, admiring the rainbow flecks.

"Elder took you to the cemetery?"

Madge nodded once.

"Good. It's important you know what's at stake."

"What does my mother have to do with it?"

"You're going to do what she couldn't." Tiger Lily lifted Madge's chin to meet her gaze. Her eyes practically glowed. "You're going to kill the Pan."

Chapter Seventeen

THE GRUMBLING, THE COMPLAINING, IT grated on Pan's nerves. Hours, they'd been searching for Madge, but they had come up with nothing to lead them to her. The wind wouldn't speak to him. The trees ignored his pleas for direction and bent away from him as if they'd rip their roots from the ground and run. What use was being the leader of an island that wouldn't obey?

Slightly lingered at the back of the group with his head down and fingered that stupid knife. Pan wanted to cut him down, lop that stupid head off his stupid shoulders. Pan's fingers tingled at the thought. But the other Lost Boys liked Slightly—almost, Pan thought, better than they liked Pan. If he wanted to keep their loyalty, Slightly had to live. For now. For a moment, Pan hoped they didn't find Madge or they found her dead. Then the Lost Boys wouldn't argue against Slightly's execution.

Whatever the result of today's search, someone was going to pay because though the others probably thought the Red Men taking Madge was a random act against Pan, he knew otherwise. Tiger Lily had been plotting against him ever since the war. Each time she attacked, he'd been one step ahead of her, thwarting her idiotic efforts and then taking one of her warriors for the trouble. They were going to try to use Madge against him. They probably showed her that ridiculous cemetery they'd been keeping.

Jane. Pan still blushed when he thought of her, and it only fueled his anger. They'd stolen her body from him. He decided to take it back.

Clouds gathered, and somewhere to the east, lightning struck.

"Uh… Pan?" Curly tapped his shoulder and pointed up. "You okay?"

Pan shook his head and took long, deep breaths. The clouds started to dissipate. "Of course I'm not okay. Mother has been taken." He glared at Slightly. "And if we don't get her back, they'll kill her."

Tootles gasped. "No!"

"We have to move faster. They've probably got her limbs roasting over a fire right now."

Jinx's face paled.

Pan resisted the urge to laugh. If only these boys knew where the meat on their feasting table *really* came from. The pig they'd caught was a happy accident. The animals had been disappearing from Neverland since before Jane arrived. The Red Men were selfish hunters; they'd see the Lost Boys starve. Lucky for them, Pan was a resourceful leader.

"I'm sure she's fine," Slightly interjected. "She's strong."

"You'd better hope so." Pan slid a finger across his throat. Pleasure radiated through his body when Slightly shuddered.

The trail picked up toward the center of the island, a mile from the tree house. It was subtle—a swatch of their red skin, dried like leather and stuck to a tree branch. They hadn't learned to fly. Pan had made sure of it. But not even Pan could navigate through the trees the way the Red Men could. No tracks. But sometimes, they got careless.

"This way," Pan said.

He wondered if Wendy had noticed Madge was missing. He wished he could sit outside her window the way he had when she was young and watch her cry over Madge's empty bed. He was almost willing to risk the few hours older he'd grow with the visit, just to see the tears slide down that ugly face.

See, Pan had chosen her. No one else could say the same. The Lost Boys he'd inherited, even the new ones. The island still called to those neglected by their parents, ignored by their family, and abandoned by anyone who'd once claimed to love them. Pan was expected to take them under his wing, to teach and guide them. But he never actually chose them.

Wendy had been different.

Her stories had called to him in his sleep. He dreamed of the adventures of Robin Hood and the nastiness of Cinderella's wicked stepmother—vivid, elaborate dreams that he knew couldn't have come from his own imagination. One night, he'd searched his dreams for their maker, and an image of Wendy—fair-haired with a stern face and piercing eyes—appeared. He knew he had to find her.

And find her he did. Pan had only ever been to the Other World once, when the Pan before him had needed help in searching for a lost boy too lost to even find Neverland. The first time Peter saw Wendy, she was telling a story about him. Peter Pan, the warrior! Peter Pan, the forever leader of Neverland!

He spent every night at her window, patiently waiting for when the stories would turn to Neverland. She knew the Lost Boys. Knew Hook. Pan had decided right away that he would have her for his own, to sing his praises and tell the boys stories.

At first, it was exactly as he'd wished. And then she'd betrayed him.

The boys' grumbling grew louder. Curly doubled over and groaned.

Pan stabbed his sword into the ground. "What now?"

Slightly stepped forward. "They're hungry."

"Seriously?"

Tootles nodded. "Diddna' even get breakfast."

Wimps, all of them. Pan reached into a satchel on his belt and pulled out one of Madge's granola bars. "No breakfast. You know, you're right, Toots."

Tootles nodded. "What with all the woosh-woosh and aahhh happenin' and all."

Pan nodded. "You're right. Which one of you boys is the hungriest, do you think?"

All hands shot in the air except Slightly's. He crossed his arms. Pan smirked.

"What do you say, boys? Think Slightly needs to eat?"

Tootles frowned. The other boys hung their heads.

Slightly straightened. "I'm fine."

"No." Pan stalked toward him, unwrapping the granola bar. It was hard, and part of it crumbled with the effort. "I think you need to eat. Tell Slightly he needs to eat, boys."

The boys' heads sank lower. A few of them nodded.

"Looks like Slightly's going to ignore my kindness. Tootles, you and Curly hold him."

They did as they were told, gripping Slightly by the arms. He was strong, but not as strong as Tootles.

"On the ground," Pan ordered.

The boys wrenched Slightly to the ground. He lashed out with his legs, but Pan jumped on top of them. Something cracked. With one hand, Pan pried open Slightly's lips. Slightly tried to bite Pan, but Slightly was too panicked and couldn't make himself focus. It was why he was a mediocre hunter. With his other hand, Pan jammed the granola bar at Slightly's teeth. They parted for an instant, and Pan rammed the bar into the back of his throat. Slightly's eyes bulged red, and he gagged. Bright yellow bile streaked from the corners of his mouth, but Pan rammed the thing further. The veins in Slightly's throat pulsed.

Tootles cleared his throat.

Curly coughed. "Pan? Sir?"

Still ramming the thing down Slightly's throat, Pan leaned down to his ear and whispered, "I want you to remember this moment. Remember who is the leader and who is the wingless fly, buzzing around my head, because I promise you, Slightly, if you so much as think about stepping out of line again, I'll smash you."

He waited for Slightly's eyes to roll back, for his struggling to slow, before he withdrew the granola bar. It took a minute for Slightly to suck in a breath.

Pan stood, leaving Tootles and Curly to help Slightly. "If you scabs are done holding us up, we continue north. There's smoke over that hill. Probably a diversion, but it's a start."

He marched forward with the boys falling in line behind him. Slightly was silent.

Chapter Eighteen

ADGE HELD THE RING so tightly it almost cut into her palm. Tiger Lily paced in front of her, a jungle cat eyeing its prey.

"I'm not doing anything," Madge said, "especially not for my kidnapper."

Tiger Lily smiled. "What loyalty do you have to Pan? Did he not kidnap you as well?"

Madge wasn't sure. She agreed to come, right? But he'd lied, or not exactly lied, but didn't tell her about her mother. She slid the ring onto her thumb—a perfect fit.

"Elder took you to the cemetery," Tiger Lily said. "What did he tell you?"

"That my mother killed herself."

She nodded. "And you don't believe that."

"I don't."

"Good. Because though she may have been the one to use the knife, Pan pushed her to do it."

"How does a boy convince a woman to kill herself? It doesn't make sense. He's just a kid."

"Pan may be a boy in body, but he is a demon in soul. His games are fueled by bloodlust. His boys murder and maim for fear of their own lives. Even his lieutenant is not safe. Pan cares for no one except himself, and damn anyone who gets in his way." Tiger Lily picked up a knife from her table. The blade glinted in the sunlight that shone through gaps in the walls. "When my father was chief of the Red Men, he watched Pan slaughter our hunters for sport, and yet he did nothing. We tear our flesh from our bodies so that the smoke might shield us as we move from place to place. But this is Pan's island. You can't hide from him here. We can't leave. So I've made the decision my father couldn't. Pan must die, and you must be the one to do it."

Madge's stomach turned. "Why?"

Tiger Lily snatched her hand with inhuman speed, stroking the opal with her finger. "Because you are a Darling. Pan has a weakness for your family."

"And why is that my problem? I came here to find my mother. I found her. There's nothing left for me here. I'm going home. You can deal with him on your own."

Tiger Lily twisted Madge's wrist, and she cried out.

"How do you expect to leave? Pan is the only person who can leave this island voluntarily. It obeys him. You're trapped, and you will do it."

"But I can't," Madge said. "I won't."

She blinked, and the knife was at her throat. Tiger Lily's face was close enough to kiss, her breath rancid from the green liquid.

"You will kill Pan, Darling. Or I will kill you."

Elder escorted Madge to the edge of the village, where a tangle of trees was all that was visible. The forest was so thick, even the sun couldn't penetrate through to the floor.

"She is under a lot of pressure," Elder said by way of apology.

Madge rubbed her neck. "She should try 'please.'"

He chuckled. "I know it doesn't seem like it now, but you are capable of doing as she asks. You're a Darling."

"It's just a last name! It has nothing to do with me or whether or not I can kill someone." And Darling was not even a name she felt belonged to her. In her own home, she'd been kept behind lock and key like a servant or a prisoner. When she was little, Madge told herself it was all a fairy tale. One day, her real mother would rescue her from the evil witch, and they'd live together, happily ever after. Darling was the name that belonged to a woman who didn't want her, not some badge of honor.

He rummaged in his robes and retrieved a yellow ribbon. "This belonged to Wendy Darling." He tied it on her wrist, stroking the ring as he finished. "She was the first to demand anything of the Pan, to stand in the way of his darkness. I believe that wish"—he tapped the ribbon—"holds some of her strength."

The ribbon was frayed at the ends and streaked with dirt, but for some reason, Madge didn't immediately want to take it off.

"You look like her," he said.

Madge had never seen a photograph of her grandmother as a girl. As far as she knew, none existed. At first, the comment stirred the already simmering blackness she felt toward Grandma Wendy. Then a traitorous thought occurred to her. If she could believe Tiger Lily and Elder, both Madge's mother and grandmother went up against Pan. Only one of them survived. Granted, looking like a young Wendy wouldn't give her boy-fighting superpowers, but maybe Grandma Wendy had known something Jane hadn't. "Where do I go? I'll get lost."

"He'll find you."

"That's what I'm afraid of."

"Don't worry. Just walk."

She walked, taking careful, short steps over the uneven ground. She turned, but the only thing she saw was the whip of Elder's silver braid disappearing into a smoky haze.

Tiger Lily slumped on the ground, drawing circles in the dirt with her knife. The blade felt loose. It'd need mending. "Come out, ghost."

The pirate, Captain Hook, appeared from the west wall. He brought with him a chill that pierced her very bones.

"Was that strictly necessary?"

She shrugged.

"I, for one, am completely in agreement that the young Miss Darling is our only hope. But she is just a girl."

"You've gone soft, Hook."

"And you, dear little Lily, have grown hard."

She stabbed the blade into the earth. "My people are dying."

"And mine are dead."

Covering her face with her hands, she took deep, measured breaths. She'd lost her center, and it was making it hard to think. Tiger Lily wasn't cruel. She'd never harm the girl. But the Pan needed to be stopped, and the girl would never take action without a push. Tiger Lily was the chief, and if she had it her way, she would be the one to drive a blade through his heart. Pan was smart, though, and would never allow her to get close enough to—whatever it took to kill an immortal boy. She'd stab him until her arms fell off if that's what it took. She'd sacrifice her own life—anything, including threatening a young girl.

Hook settled next to her. "Sulk later. Tell me, do the Red Men ever settle near the island's edge?"

She dropped her hands. "If necessary."

"Time to pack up, then."

"Why?"

"A hunch."

She snorted. "I will not uproot my people on the whim of a ghost."

"Then uproot them for the sake of their lives. Pan will find Madge and then... what? You think he'll let this little stunt go unpunished?"

Reluctantly, she nodded. "We'll leave at dusk."

"Good. In the meantime, a plan needs forming."

"I have a plan." Tiger Lily pointed her blade to the place where Madge had stood. "The girl will kill him."

"How?"

She fell silent.

"Tell me, dear." He lowered his face to meet hers. Such close proximity to the dead unsettled her. "Did you notice that upon returning from Madge's world, Pan had grown?"

From the diary of Wendy Moira Angela Darling

I am so tired, Diary, tired of fighting for something that is so obviously no longer mine. The princess is out of the picture now—Peter's treaty torn to pieces—but it has done nothing to bring him closer to me. Peter is in love with himself. How can I compete with that?

John, too, is tiring of Neverland. While the others lose themselves in the hunt or gutting an animal for a feast (the nightly feasts!), John sequesters himself in a corner of the tree house, humming a slow melody. Peter ignores him, which, given the alternative of his wrath, is fine. Part of me feels guilty at having brought them in the first place. They wanted to come, I tell myself. But I know they wouldn't have come on their own.

Michael whimpers in his sleep, calls for Mother. I hold him during the worst of these fits, but I can't help resenting his loyalty to the red princess. He asks about her often. Doesn't he realize how it pains me? Does no one on this godforsaken island care about my happiness?

Today, I thought things were changing. Peter brought me to see the fairies—what beauty!—and for a moment, it felt like we would return to the beginning. As the fairy melody reached its peak, Peter looked at me with eyes a husband lays on his wife, and my heart fluttered like the thousands of fairy wings. He kissed me, and I tasted his salty-sweet mouth. I could have cried for the joy it brought me.

But it was not to be.

Again, he pulled away. Was it shame he felt? Anger at his yearning? I wish I could convince him that it's a good and normal thing, but he won't listen.

"It's time for spring cleaning," he said.

And I can't help wondering, Diary, what cleaning will fix. It certainly did my mother no good. I can tell you, though, that if he thinks I'll be doing all of the work, he's got another think coming.

Chapter Nineteen

KILL PETER PAN.

Madge tromped through the brush, heart hammering harder. With each scrape of a branch and unnerving twitch of a bird's head up in the trees, she became more convinced that she might not have a choice. She'd been recruited—no, ordered—to assassinate a person who, for all intents and purposes, shouldn't even exist.

But how could she even consider killing someone? There was no question she had it in her. Given the right circumstances, everyone could kill another person. She believed that. What she couldn't believe, though, was what Tiger Lily had said about her mother. Madge had been too young when her mother disappeared to remember much about her, but she felt, deep down in her heart, that her mother wouldn't have killed herself, wouldn't take herself away from Madge permanently. That meant she'd been murdered. The question: who? Tiger Lily was the one who'd had Jane's ring and ruled over the village that kept her body under the ground. Maybe the Red Men had killed her. Maybe they were to blame for it all. Maybe it was they who were evil.

Madge held on to this thought, twirling the ring around her finger. The sound of a crow echoed behind the trees.

"She's close," Pan said.

Slightly allowed himself the briefest moment of relief. Maybe he wouldn't have to die after all. Most importantly, Madge was probably safe.

Nibs sniffed the air. "I don' smell nuffin'."

Slightly elbowed the kid in the chest. "Shut up."

"Don' get mad at me. You're the one who screwed everyfin' up."

"I didn't screw up."

"Mm-hmm. You screwed up," Tootles added.

Slightly tightened a fist only to have it smacked away by Pan. "Quiet."

Slightly nodded. It'd been a long morning made longer by the fact that night didn't get a chance to finish. No one had slept, and it showed on Slightly more than the others. He wouldn't dare complain, however.

Above them, a pair of Neverbirds pecked and squawked over what was left of some kind of rodent. Pan stopped suddenly. Flicking his gaze upward, he launched a rock. It smacked into one of the birds with an audible crunch. The victor climbed into the sky with his prize.

Tootles pouted. "I liked the blue one."

"Keep moving." Pan reared back and crowed, quickening his pace.

The boys ran behind him with Slightly at the tail. The only sound was the crunch of twigs beneath their feet and the wind past his ears. To his left, something cracked. If he investigated and found nothing, Pan would have Slightly's head for abandoning the hunt. If none of them found anything, Pan would have Slightly's head anyway. Slightly veered to the left, careful not to alert whatever it was to his presence. He'd had enough encounters with saber tigers to know they pounced when spooked.

Yellow blooms turned their faces his way as he sneaked past. One oozed red, and he shuddered. Of all the things he'd seen in Neverland, the flesh-eating flowers were the ones that never sat right with him. Wasn't natural.

Pan's crow faded behind him, but the rustle ahead grew. The trees were packed against each other, making it difficult to see further than a foot or so. A flash of black. A squeal.

Slightly's chest tightened. He hurdled over rocks toward the sound. "Madge?"

A scream. He ran, hoping against hope it wasn't a saber. In the chaos of the search, Slightly lost his spear.

He slid through a net of vines and saw her cowering against a tree. He followed her gaze and laughed. "It's a mouse."

The creature flicked its tail, and Madge shrieked. "It's got pointy teeth!"

Slightly rolled his eyes. Girls. He stomped close to the mouse. "Shoo! Go on!"

It skittered away, disappearing behind a log.

Madge straightened, and Slightly noticed she wore Red Man robes and a belt cinched tightly around her waist. It didn't look terrible. Around her wrist was a nappy ribbon. He recognized it immediately as the one that Wendy had worn in her hair. If Pan saw it... Slightly didn't notice her body shivering until he stepped closer.

"Had a bit of an adventure, eh?"

Her gaze was fixed on the ribbon. She didn't say anything.

He leaned in, knowing Pan had ears everywhere, and whispered, "Don't let him see the ribbon."

She met his gaze, at first icy, then softer. She untied it and stuffed it in the folds of her robe.

Slightly offered a small smile before calling out, "Pan! I've found her!"

The sound was like a stampede—quick, angry footfalls crushing everything in their path. Crows and cries echoed louder until they vibrated in her chest. Madge twisted the opal to face inward so that only the silver band was visible. If she wasn't supposed to let Pan see the ribbon, he probably shouldn't see the ring, either.

He emerged, red-faced, with bits of green stuck in his hair and on his clothes. Dirt slashed his face like a scar. The others fell in behind him, huffing and holding their sides. At first, Pan smiled. As he took in her appearance—oiled skin and Red Man robes—he frowned, though the expression didn't look much different.

"Are you okay?" he asked.

Slightly was quick to answer for her. "She's fine."

Madge nodded. Her voice was buried beneath the images of Pan holding a knife to her mother's gut the way Madge had held it to his the night they'd met.

Pan jumped and stood in front of her. He gripped her chin and yanked it to the right, exposing her neck. It stung like a partially healed cut ripped open.

"They hurt you."

She tried to shake her head, but his grip held. Tiger Lily had probably nicked her. "I'm fine."

He dropped her chin. She thought she caught the hint of a smile on his face.

Turning to the Lost Boys, he said, "The Red Men have hurt Mother! Will we stand for this?"

"No!" they cried in unison.

Madge rubbed her throbbing jaw, flinching at the pain. There would be a bruise.

"Onward, men! We shall avenge Mother!"

The Lost Boys whooped and waved their weapons. Slightly stood quietly beside her.

Pan turned to him, hand resting on the knife at his hip. His smile was all teeth. "You'll escort Mother back to the house. Try not to lose her again."

Slightly opened his mouth but thought better of it.

Panic fluttered in Madge's chest. They couldn't possibly find the camp, right? That was what Elder had said. No, he'd said it didn't always work. Tiger Lily could handle herself. Madge wasn't particularly worried about the chief anyway, but the others... And it would be her fault. But he wouldn't actually *kill* them, would he?

Grandma Wendy had stood up to him. That was what that pirate had said. Was Madge brave enough to do the same?

"Peter," she said, hoping to appeal to whatever humanity was left inside him.

He ignored her, starting back the way she'd come.

She pinched her palm. Breathed. "Peter!"

He stopped but didn't turn. "Yes, Mother?"

Tiger Lily said her family had a hold on him. Maybe... "Whatever you're thinking of doing. Don't. I'm fine."

"Oooo," the fat one said.

Slightly's eyes widened.

Pan turned his head, eyes narrowed. "That's not the rules to this game, girl. You're Mother. That makes me Father. And Mother must always obey Father, mustn't she?"

The Lost Boys nodded enthusiastically.

Slightly hung his head.

"That's not—" Madge started.

"My game. My rules." Pan turned to the boys. "To war!"

"To war!"

"War!"

"War on!"

She tried to shout over them, but Pan's crow drowned out her voice. Blades the size of their forearms punched the air. They ran, wolves on the hunt.

Chapter Twenty

SLIGHTLY GRABBED HER HAND AND started walking. "Come on."
Madge pulled her hand away but followed, putting her feet
where he stepped. "We have to stop him."

Snort. "Ain't no stopping Pan once he decides something."

"And you just do whatever he tells you?"

He shrugged.

"Coward."

He wheeled around, face red. "I didn't see you running off to stop
him, did I?"

"I tried," she said with more conviction in her heart than her voice.
"And anyway, he'd listen to you before he'd listen to me."

"No, he wouldn't." His gaze fell briefly to the ground.

"I know he would."

Slightly shook his head, turning back to the path. "You don't
know anything."

"If you would just—"

"Do all girls talk this much, or just you *Darlings*?"

She fell silent, but part of her was tempted to list every item in her
grandmother's house, out loud, in pig Latin.

As they continued through the trees, Slightly marched confidently
while Madge struggled to recognize anything. She strained to hear any
sign that Pan had reached the camp. Every bird caw was his crow and
the rustle of squirrels a scuffle. She thought she heard a scream but
convinced herself it was her imagination.

Soon, the smell of saltwater hit her nose.

"I thought we were going to the tree house."

"We are."

"I smell the ocean."

"It's an island."

She rolled her eyes. "Yeah, but when we were at the tree house before, I didn't smell the ocean. Where are we?"

"Fekkin' girls. Always ruining everything," he muttered. "We'll go to the tree house. I want to make a stop first."

They veered left on a less obvious path, and the ground turned soft. A gull flew overhead, and the saltwater scent grew stronger. She heard rushing water and something that sounded like a downpour. The trees thinned the further they walked until there was nothing but rocks and sand and sky and ocean. The water was sapphire blue and sparkled like a billion gemstones. Waves crashed against the shoreline, which cut in a wide arc until it reached a stone cave. Water trickled over the mouth like a curtain.

This was the magic of Neverland. As her eyes drank in every color, every glittering fleck of light on the water, Madge ignored all her anxieties about the Red Men and Pan and her family. A cool breeze trickled through, drying the sweat on Madge's neck and forehead. She approached the water, eager to rinse her feet and hands. Something splashed nearby.

"Don't get too close," Slightly said.

"Why?"

Another splash. Then a creature burst from the water, tail long and glistening, with the torso and upper body of a woman. Her hair was as green as her fin and whipped over her face as she dove.

"Those aren't..."

Slightly smirked. "Mermaids."

Madge took a step toward the water, but Slightly snatched her back by her robe.

"I mean it. Not too close. They don't like it when we go in there."

She nodded and gazed across the ocean. She saw flashes of green and flickers of fins. "Are they dangerous?"

"Just territorial."

"Then why'd you bring me here?"

"It's nice to look at, I guess? I don't know. Just seemed like you needed something to look at." Cheeks pink and jaw working around some unsaid something, he picked up a rock and skipped it over the surface. Webbed hands shot up out of the water. One caught it. "Used to come here a lot when I first got to Neverland."

"When was that?"

He shrugged.

"Long time?"

"Yeah."

Once her eyes left the water, Madge's fears and anxieties came rushing back. How long was long, and how could she possibly know if Pan controlled the measure of days? She wanted to go home, but at the same time, she knew what waited for her there—Grandma Wendy and her half-truths. She sat on the sand, thankful for the warmth on her aching legs and feet. She'd walked more in the last few days than the last year combined.

"Nibs and Tootles and them weren't here yet. I was first."

"Before Pan?"

He chuckled. "No. No one was before Pan."

"How did he get here, then?"

"Depends on who you ask. Pan says he climbed out of his pram when he heard his folks getting all excited about his future, and then the fairies hauled him off to Neverland. The fairies say he sprouted out of one of those yellow lilies, but they wouldn't claim him, would they? Hook said he came from the deepest pits of Hell..."

"And you?"

Slightly didn't answer. His gaze narrowed over the water to where two pairs of slitted eyes peered from just above the surface. As they drew closer, they rose out of the water—green, algae-like hair that clung to the mermaids' backs, humanoid torsos as slick and leathery as shark's skin. Madge couldn't tear her eyes from the way their bodies slinked across the water, barely registering a ripple on the surface. They stopped about ten feet from the shore. One turned her eyes toward Madge. A song with a melody both sweet and heart wrenching swirled through her mind, and her vision went black at the corners. She knew she had to get in the water. Nothing would make her happy like the water and all its many gifts. She fell on all fours, inching forward.

Slightly stepped in front of her. "She's Pan's."

Suddenly, the melody was gone. She looked up at Slightly, but his eyes were fixed on the mermaids. His arms hung stiff at his sides.

The mermaid on the left spoke, and her voice sounded garbled, like someone speaking underwater. "Tell Pan we've found a ship."

Slightly nodded. Madge couldn't tell if this was good news or bad. "Tell him it will cost him."

The one on the right added, "Tell him it will cost him double."

Slightly nodded again.

Madge blinked, and the mermaids were gone. "Cost him double what?"

His face turned gray. He shook his head and offered his hand. "We need to get to the tree house."

Madge stood and followed but couldn't stop looking over her shoulder. The hair on her neck stood on end, and shivers plowed down her spine. She knew it was a stupid question, but asked anyway. "Should I be scared?"

Slightly reached behind and grabbed her hand, squeezing it once before letting go.

Tiger Lily rested on her haunches, peering through a gap in the rocks. "You were right."

Hook huffed. "Could you sound more surprised?"

"Hush, phantom."

Goose bumps trailed the length of Tiger Lily's arms. She smelled it on the wind—something was wrong.

"The only variable is, of course, the girl. She's no Wendy, I'll admit. But I think—"

"I said, hush!"

She stood, closing her eyes. Something cold brushed the back of her neck, and her mind filled with so many screams.

"Dear Lord," Hook whispered.

Her eyes snapped open. Pan's shadow rippled in the wind before flying off in the distance.

Panic seized her chest. "No."

A strangled cry escaped her lips, and then she ran.

Chapter Twenty-One

I T WAS ALL TOO RED. Too loud. And all too bloody familiar.
Hook watched from atop a bluff while below, Pan and the Lost
Boys slaughtered Tiger Lily's people like animals. The older boys
tore through the camp, slashing anything in their paths, wearing freshly
shorn scalps, braids swinging like pendulums.

Tick-tock, tick-tock.

Hook had experienced the sensation of time slowing as an enemy
descended, teeth-bared and growling, before. Then a blink, and it
was over.

But this seemed never ending.

Tiger Lily pounced on Pan each time his feet touched solid ground,
but he was like lightning. He laughed, waggling his tongue at her with
every missed swing. Her cries reached Hook's ears, even way up here on
the bluff.

The boys fought without skill—all elbows and thrashing knives—
but they struck more than they missed. Their crude blades made of
stone and rusted metal took jagged chunks out of thighs and stomachs.
The big, oafish one, Tootles, sliced a woman's nose clean off her face.

Hook shook his head. *Kill the men if you must,* he thought, *but
women have no place at the pointed end of a sword.*

The sun blazed brighter, hotter. Clouds fizzled in the brightness,
putting a spotlight on the battle. The jungle behind Hook quieted. He
spotted a vulture poised at the base of a tree, head slightly angled toward
the fight as though intrigued by the stench of raw meat.

An arrow flew through the edge of Hook's shoulder. One of the Lost Boys saluted—his hand covered in blood—before returning to the fray.

"Never thought you'd be glad to be already dead, did ye, Cap'n?" Smee sat on the edge of the bluff, phantasmal legs dangling over the side.

"No, Smee. I didn't."

In truth, Hook would have given anything to be able to charge down into the camp and take his due, not out of loyalty to the Red Men—they'd done nothing for him—but just to get the chance to hack both hands from Pan's body and toss them to the mermaids.

The battle raged on, even as the Red Men tired and the boys were forced to climb over the bodies they felled.

"Would've made a good pirate." Smee nodded in Pan's direction.

Hook snarled. "There is honor even amongst thieves, Smee. That foul creature is better fit to fertilize the bottom of the ocean than to sail one."

Smee lowered his head. "Aye, Cap'n."

The fighting had slowed. Women of the Red Men camp frantically dragged their dead into their huts now that the boys had lost interest in them. A young girl sobbed over the body of a man, distinguishable only by his masculine chest. His face was smashed to meat pulp, and his legs were gone. Most of the Lost Boys helped to drag a pair of their comrades into the jungle.

Tiger Lily stood in the middle of the carnage, arms stiff at her sides. She glanced up at Hook and shook her head. She was disappointed in him. One more burden she needn't have borne. But what could he have possibly done?

Pan approached Tiger Lily. Sheathed his dagger. "I think we're done here."

"Impossible. You're still alive," Tiger Lily said through clenched teeth.

He sighed. "You still don't get it, princess. I *am* Neverland. As long as there's an island, there will be Peter Pan. You could stab me through the heart with that pathetic little spear you've got there, and I would still live."

Her lip twitched. "Prove it."

"You'd like that, wouldn't you?"

"More than you know."

"Oh, I know, princess. See, you cut a piece off of my girl. By all rights, I should cut a chunk from you. Maybe one of those pretty golden eyes."

Tiger Lily snorted. "Your girl? Madge? Think again, Pan. She's going to ask you about Jane. We both know what happened, and your ego won't let you lie about it."

He shrugged and turned away.

She spit in the dirt. "This isn't over."

He glanced over his shoulder. Smiled. "I sure hope not."

Don't leave town, they'd told him. Michael had laughed. Where could he possibly go? He had every intention of going back to his shitty apartment to drown himself in cheap whiskey, but he found himself in Wendy's driveway. He killed the engine and stared at the house for a while. The windows were still lit up. He allowed himself a moment of hope that Madge had come home, that it was all a giant misunderstanding.

But Michael knew better. Pan didn't just let people go. Not anymore.

The stench of booze and old vomit hit him like a wall as soon as he opened the door. He left it open to air the place out a bit and covered the worst of the mess with a sheet from the closet.

At first, Michael had loved Pan. They all did, of course, but Michael especially. John wasn't a terrible big brother, but his interests had been in giant books of ancient history that Michael found incredibly dull. As a boy, all Michael had cared about were games, especially pirate games. Pan had said those were his favorite too.

But Pan's definition of *game* was loose and dangerous. Michael's greatest dream came true when he boarded a real pirate ship and spoke to real pirates. The captain, Hook, looked every bit as fearsome as Bluebeard. Michael's body had vibrated with excitement. He'd had so many questions.

The fighting began almost instantly. Michael hadn't known what was happening until Slightly's sword clanged against the sword of a pirate directly over Michael's head. He'd panicked, crying for Wendy, but she'd been left at the tree house. Somehow, he'd managed to crawl into a space between gunpowder barrels without being hit. He'd hid so long he pissed his pants.

Pan had killed them all that day. All of Michael's beloved pirates.

Now, he climbed the stairs up to Wendy's room. The bed was made, lavender duvet spread evenly across the mattress. The scent of powder and fabric softener enveloped him as he lay on top of the duvet. He didn't want to mess it up by climbing beneath the covers. First, he would take those damned bars off of Madge's window—in case of a miracle. Then, he would sleep.

When he finally fell asleep, hands cut up and covered in plaster dust, he dreamed of Neverland. He was small again and chased a squirrel through the jungle. It had Michael's stuffed penguin, and he wanted it back. Wendy appeared, blocking his path. When she looked at him, it was her old-woman face on her young-girl body. Tears stung Michael's eyes.

"What's wrong with you?" he asked.

Her face changed. She was Jane, blood blossoming from her stomach. She was Madge, shaking her head. Her eyes rolled back into her skull, and she fell backward into a pit. Michael stood on the edge, too scared to reach in, too scared even to call her name.

"Hello, Michael," Pan said from behind him.

Michael turned, and Pan snatched his hand. In one smooth stroke, Pan cut off Michael's fingers.

Pan sent the boys ahead to the tree house, saying he needed to take care of the bodies. With the frenzy of the battle over, the Lost Boys were all too happy to leave him to the task. It was one thing to play war, another to deal with the consequences. He was impressed they'd only lost Patches and Rudy. Going into battle was always a risk—lose too many of his men and he risked his own life—but it was a risk he was willing to take for Madge's honor.

Patches was basically just a torso now with a bit of leg flesh still dangling from one side. His head was attached by his throat rope, and it flopped as Pan dragged his body to a secluded part of the jungle. Rudy was whole, but he'd taken a spear to the chest and a hatchet to the temple. It was like his body was painted with blood, and it smeared over Pan's face as he undressed the boy. Using his fingers, he palpitated Rudy's leg and arm flesh. Muscly, but still with a little baby fat on the undersides. Patches was fatter, and Pan wished he'd had the time to find Patches' legs.

Oh well, he thought. *Waste not.*

With an expert hand, Peter sliced his sharpened knife along Rudy's leg, separating the flesh from the bone. Most of the tendons cut away easily, but a bit of muscle snagged on his knife, and he hacked away at it until half of the filet was mutilated. Not unusable, but wholly unappetizing. Once the good parts were cut from both boys, Pan skinned them, packing those bits in a separate sack to give to Snowball later. The rest—bones and innards—Pan left for the scavengers.

He should've killed Tiger Lily while he'd had the chance. The mistake nagged at him as he marched toward the tree house. He'd underestimated her before and vowed not to make the same mistake again. She'd mass new troops, come back stronger than ever. He could take her. Pan had no doubt. But what of his men? If any more of them fell to her before Pan had a chance to bring more to the island...

No. He wouldn't let it happen. Neverland simply couldn't exist without him.

From the diary of Wendy Moira Angela Darling

This was my last chance, Diary.

Something has happened, something Peter assures me is vital to the continuance of the existence of Neverland. Dutiful, obedient wife, I promised to assist in any way I could.

You are just a collection of my thoughts, but I still feel compelled to explain myself, perhaps to explain myself to myself. To justify my actions. It seems that's all I do lately—explain away my deeds as unavoidable.

Anyway.

It seems that Neverland's power cannot stave off time forever. Moments pass, and the boys age in tiny increments. In order to keep the power of the island alive, the oldest of the boys must be sacrificed. I'm frightened as I write this. To see the words tumble out of me and onto paper is to make it real.

They braided the rope from the scalps of slaughtered Red Men. John tied the noose. He's become silent. Quiet acquiescence is his only action. Whatever damage has been done to his mind, I'm worried it may be permanent.

I'm pausing in the narrative to commit to paper the goodness in one of the boys. Jolly is... was... a good boy. At this point, it's the only repentance I can give. The boy smiled when no one else could, loved every grain of sand on the island. His laugh always drew the attention of a badger that poked its head from the earth whenever he laughed. He was lovely.

And I told him his favorite story—the Pied Piper—as a barrel was kicked from beneath his feet, and the rope snapped his small neck.

Don't hate me, Diary.

I finished the story even as he swung, lifeless. His soul deserved the peace that comes with a happy ending.

Michael ran for Jolly's feet (how he'd looked up to that boy), tears streaming down his fat face. Before I could reach him, Pan snatched Michael from the ground. They flew out of sight, and when they returned, Michael was missing two fingers.

It's my fault.

I've had enough.

We must leave Neverland.

Chapter Twenty-Two

I T WAS WARM IN THE tree house. Slightly offered Madge a pair of shorts and a shirt that appeared to be about a million years old.
"Whose are these?"

He shrugged and turned around so she could change.

The shorts fit, but the shirt was long, hanging like a nightgown. Not much to look at, but she felt more like herself.

Slightly bundled the Red Man robe and stuffed it at the bottom of a pile of rags. "You should get some rest."

"I'm not tired." She was tired, but her mind was a mess. Tiger Lily. Madge's mother. Pan's threat to avenge a stupid scratch on her neck and the sickening idea that they were all connected.

"Still."

"What are you going to do?"

He flopped at the base of a large root and withdrew a small hunk of wood and a knife from beneath a bunk. "Wait."

She looked from him to her bunk—Wendy's bunk—and back again. "You knew my grandmother. She was here."

Slightly carved at the hunk of wood, eyebrows furrowed.

"Was my mother here too?" She loomed over him, daring him to say no. "Don't lie to me."

Curlicues of wood littered his lap. His mouth twisted, and he bowed low over his work.

She'd seen that look before. Uncle Michael wore it whenever she pressed about his fingers or her mother or anything about his life before she was born. He'd thought he was protecting her. Look where all that protection had brought her.

She leaned in close to Slightly's ear. "You're just like him, aren't you? All that 'let's show Madge the ocean and the trees' crap was just a front, wasn't it?"

He threw the wooden thing across the room, and it bounced off a bunk, splitting in two. "Why does it matter? Huh? It won't help you to know. It won't help anyone. And even if I wanted to tell you, which I don't, I couldn't. Okay? Do you get it?"

She clenched her jaw until it hurt. "I deserve to know."

A sudden chill filled the room, and something dark passed overhead.

Slightly scrambled to his feet and slapped a hand over her mouth. "Not another word about it. Hear me? Or would you rather see me killed?"

She flinched as the bruise on her cheek throbbed.

He pulled away, stuffing his hands in his pockets. His voice dropped to a whisper. "You know they were here. Then they weren't. End of story."

"But how—"

Shaking his head, he returned to his place on the floor and retrieved another hunk of wood from under the bunk. "They left. If you're smart, you'll leave too. Eventually."

"How?"

He didn't answer.

She sighed. "And until then?"

"Play the game."

"What if I don't want to?"

He smiled, but it didn't reach his eyes. "You really are a Darling. Through and through."

"Thank you. I guess."

His face fell. "It wasn't a compliment."

It was a long time before Pan and his Lost Boys returned to the tree house. Slightly stayed silent the entire time, digging notches into his piece of wood, while Madge struggled to sleep. She pressed her body against the wall of the tree house only to feel Slightly's eyes on her back. She wanted to believe it was out of concern, his constant staring, but part of her suspected otherwise. Pan had tasked him with "making sure she didn't get lost again." She was his responsibility. Madge didn't want to think of what would happen to him—and her—if she wandered off. This kept her in the bunk, struggling to sleep because, as much as Slightly might not have seemed to care much about telling her what she needed to know, she was beginning to care about him. He was kind in his own way.

Madge felt the Lost Boys' return before she heard it. She was on the edge of sleep when her bunk vibrated in a *thump-thump* rhythm. The boys were marching home.

She turned over, and Slightly was on his feet, wooden trinket and knife hidden back beneath the bunk.

"They put away?" he asked, and she knew he meant her ring and ribbon.

She stuffed them in her pocket just as a door burst open and a chant filled the tree house:

"Dead Red Men!
Dead Red Men!
Dead Red Men!"

Bile rose to the top of her throat, and she struggled to swallow it back down.

No.

They couldn't have.

Her hands shook, and she stuffed them beneath her thighs to hide them.

The boys gathered in the center of the room carrying sacks, some with bloodstains at the bottom. Their faces were covered in mud and red and slashed by crazed smiles. Pan entered at the end, and they all cheered. Madge bit her lip to keep from screaming. On his head was a gray scalp, long braid swinging mournfully behind.

"Let us celebrate," Pan said, "for Mother has been avenged!"

Madge lurched upright and threw her legs over the side of the bunk. Swirling fury built in her chest. She wanted to throw things, to scream, to smash everything in the tree house. "I didn't want this."

Pan laughed, his eyes wide and wild. "You're a girl. Girls don't know what they want."

"I do," she said through clenched teeth. "So did my mother and grandmother, didn't they? That's why Grandma Wendy left, wasn't it? Why my mother is buried on this island instead of back in my world, alive? Because of you. Because they couldn't stand to be near you anymore."

The room fell quiet. She straightened, vowing not to shrivel beneath his stare. *You'll blink first*, she thought.

Slightly positioned himself between them, cutting off the contest. "The mermaids have found you a ship."

Like a gnat, Pan's attention flitted away from Madge. He smiled, all trace of anger wiped clean. "Wonderful!"

"They want double pay."

The boys seemed to shrink before her eyes. Gone were the warrior expressions, replaced by little boys worried about being caught with their hands in the cookie jar.

Pan scowled, but only for an instant. "Fish-maids always demand more than they're due. But I must have a ship, so double they'll get." His gaze found Madge. "And Mother will choose the payment."

"Me?" Madge's body burned under his stare. "Why?"

"Choose, Mother."

"How?"

"I'm glad you asked." He ripped the scalp from his head and tossed it in a heap at her feet. It looked and smelled like roadkill. "Boys, line up." He turned to Slightly, whispering just loud enough for Madge to hear. "You too, lover boy."

Slightly's cheeks turned angry red, and he fell in line with the others. Pan walked past them, humming and slashing their foreheads with stripes of blood pulled from a puddle that formed beneath one of the bags. He turned to Madge and offered his hand. She climbed down without touching him and stood just out of grabbing distance.

He drove his heel in the ground, creating a divot in the dirt. "You stand here."

She obeyed.

He blindfolded her with a dirty rag. The stench made her gag.

"Careful now, Mother. We don't want to get vomit on the floor."

Footsteps around her. Some were close, some far away. They didn't stop moving until Pan told them to. Then there was a heavy silence.

He placed his lips to Madge's ear. "Turn twice, and then point. Then do it again."

"What happens then?"

No answer, only a hand like a vise on her arm, and then she was spinning on her heel. Something caught her ankle, and she stopped.

"Point," Pan said.

She lifted her arm and pointed directly in front of her.

The silence deepened. Someone sniffed, then there was the thump of fist on soft flesh.

"Again," Pan said.

He shoved her shoulder, and she spun until he kicked her ankle.

"Point."

Again, she lifted her hand and pointed directly in front of her. The rag lifted a touch, and she saw small boy feet back away, toes curled.

"There," Pan said. "That wasn't so hard, was it?"

Without being told, she ripped the putrid thing from her eyes and breathed deeply the smell of boy and dirt and flowers. Slightly stood to her left, half hidden behind a knot in the tree. She thought she saw his shoulders heave once before he straightened. She glanced around and noticed there were fewer boys than before. The small one, Curly, was missing. So was the quiet one. Madge couldn't remember his name.

"When do we go?" Slightly asked.

Pan slapped his back. "You don't go anywhere. Madge and I will head out at dawn. Tonight, we tell stories of our great victory over the Red Man!"

The Lost Boys lifted their fists, but their cries were cheerless. Sunlight paled with dizzying speed until the fragments of light through the trees were black. Nighttime. Better for storytelling, Pan insisted.

There was a feast, and though Madge was starving, she didn't touch a bite for fear of what was inside. Other than a few snide remarks—*ungrateful, how dare she?*—Pan left her to sulk. Curly and the quiet one weren't at the table, their empty places marked with giant nothings around them. Tootles shot nasty looks at Madge from time to time, but only when there wasn't any food on his plate.

Slightly sat next to her. "Curly's his best friend."

"I still don't understand what's happening."

"What's happening," Pan said, "is the assured, continued existence of Neverland."

Slightly turned to his plate where a chop of something sat, still rare and bloody. He poked at it then slipped a piece the size of a thumbnail past his lips.

Madge dumped hers in the dirt and covered it with leaves. She'd had enough blood to last a hundred lifetimes. How much had her mother seen? Grandma Wendy? In her world, people died every day, and the news stations made sure everyone heard about it. But even though she knew these boys and the Red Men about as well as she knew the strangers on the news, this felt closer. Hit harder. Who could choose to live this way? Her gaze drifted to the jungle. When she'd first arrived, it'd seemed so alive. Now, it was desolate and ugly. Shadows haunted the trees, and she could swear one stared at her from the lower branches of a banana tree.

She wanted to go home.

Pan launched into the air to begin his tale. He brought with him a ball of flame that twisted like a globe, and as he spoke, it morphed into shapes to illustrate his words. Even though the boys had all witnessed the event firsthand, they were enthralled. Their jaws slackened, and their eyes widened and glazed. They loved him, worshiped him like some terrible god. In her heart, Madge didn't blame them. Pan was charismatic and evil, and they loved him.

The ball of fire spread wings and a tail. Light flickered over Pan's body, making it look as though he moved in slow motion. "I followed the phoenix. She is the only bird of her kind in Neverland and belongs to Chief Tiger Lily."

Tootles booed.

"Yes! What right do the Red Men have to possess such a beautiful creature of the sky when they're cursed to the ground?"

"None!" the boys shouted. They sat up straighter. Nibs nibbled an ear of purple corn without blinking.

The fire spread wide like a projection and then split, dividing into characters as Pan described the slaughter. Madge clutched her stomach, unable to look away. Even as fiery silhouettes, she recognized the woman who'd cleaned her, the boy who'd peeked through the door at her, Elder...

"For refusing to join us," Pan said as an afterthought, "and for hurting Mother, I was forced to remind him of the power of the Pan."

Fire-Pan raised his machete as real-Pan raised his.

Madge shoved away from the table, knocking over cups and saucers, and ran.

Chapter Twenty-Three

I T WAS LIKE THE STUPID girl wanted him dead.

Slightly ran after her, but the path she took was erratic, and in the dark it was near impossible to see. Soon, the crunch of leaves stopped, and he had nothing to follow.

Then the birds. God, the screeching. They only got riled like that if there was a predator. Slightly cursed and sprinted toward the sound, thankful he'd remembered his knife this time.

He found Madge behind a willow, clutching her stomach.

"You've got to stop doing that," he said.

The next few seconds flicked past in slow motion. She was behind the willow then in his face. Something hard connected with the side of his head, and he hit the ground.

"Ungh..." His head spun.

"Isn't that how you people talk around here?" She threw dead leaves and twigs at his face. "Pain and violence, right? That's how I get my point across? I have to hurt you?"

"Stop."

"Why?" More leaves. A few small rocks. One dinged his nose. He was pretty sure he was bleeding.

He turned over, covering his head with his hands. The girl was crazy. *All* girls were crazy. Stupid girls with their feelings and their faces and their eyes. Green eyes. He held his breath as an image crept to the surface. Green eyes and pink cheeks. Mouth wide and yelling. What'd he do this time? A smaller girl version of the first, laughing. His mind gave them names.

Slightly froze, his mouth forming the words again, to give them shape: my mother and sister.

Then out loud. "My mother and sister."

"What?" She huffed. Coughed.

He sat up, meeting her gaze. "My mother and sister."

"What about them? You kill them too?"

"No, I... I had them. I had a mother and sister."

Madge slouched. The fight sloughed out of her body but not her eyes.

Slightly closed his eyes, digging his fists into them to keep the images in his mind. A woman with blond hair tied tight above her head looking at him with smiling green eyes, a girl two years his senior, a miniature version of their mother, but with one brown eye and one blue. He recited their names, "Mary and Elizabeth, Mary and Elizabeth," etching them in his brain and his mouth.

He finally opened his eyes. They were still there. His family existed. They were real. And his name wasn't Slightly.

"Edward," he whispered.

Madge sank next to him and placed her hand on his. "Nice to meet you, Eddy."

"Edward. Not Eddy."

She shook her head. "Nope. Edward is a stupid name. Eddy is better."

He grinned. Eddy wasn't so bad.

She frowned, pulling out the ring he knew belonged to Jane. Jane had showed it to him once. She was proud of it.

"Eddy, what happened to my mom?"

He paused. Tell, and Pan would have his head. But Pan would think of a reason to have his head anyway. Slightly wasn't stupid. He was a threat. Pan didn't waste time dealing with threats.

"At first," Slightly began, "Pan brought Jane to Neverland to get back at Wendy. In his own twisted way, he was fond of Wendy and took it hard when she left."

Madge scooted closer. "Why did she leave?"

He shrugged. "Who knows? But when she decided to leave, Pan didn't argue. He was confident she'd come back. And she did, once, but then she swore to stay away. Jane was supposed to remind Wendy of what she'd left behind."

"What happened?"

"Same thing that happened the first time, I guess. Jane was different than Wendy—quieter. At first, Pan didn't like how soft she was on the boys. She'd knit things for them. Mend pockets and stuff. Then she and Pan got real close." Slightly blushed, thinking of the acts he'd walked in on. The nakedness. "Then something happened, and he sent her away for a while. She came back different. Angrier. Pan didn't like that."

Madge's voice softened. "He killed her."

"No. She killed herself."

"But Tiger Lily said—"

"I never said it wasn't Pan's fault. He has this way with people. It's like they fall under some kind of spell and do exactly what he wants them to, no matter what."

"Even you?"

Slightly clicked his tongue. Enough truth for one day. "We should get back."

"Someone needs to do something," Madge said, almost to herself.

Slightly patted her shoulder, offering a small smile. He knew there was nothing anyone could do against Pan without getting themselves killed. Or worse.

Although…

He hadn't been lying when he'd told Pan that Madge was different. Maybe she'd be different enough.

Chapter Twenty-Four

Once upon a time...

CREW SLAUGHTERED. HOOK, A SPECTRAL mirror of his former self, bound to Neverland forever. It couldn't get any worse. And then it did.

Never one to stay land-bound for long, Hook boarded the *Jolly Roger* as a ghost in mourning, unable to caress her bannisters or grip her wheel with a firm but gentle hand. Her sails drooped sadly, and her planks still bore the gore of the fight. She was quiet. Still. Funereal. There had only been one other occasion that pricked the black heart of Captain Hook—a girl, a promise, a betrayal—but knowing his ship was vulnerable to the likes of Peter Pan... Hook could have wept.

Since ghosts did not weep, he chose instead to pace her deck and remember the feel of the wind and spray of the sea on his face as he barked orders to his loyal crew. And they had been loyal, up until the end. Hook had failed them a second time. Perhaps that was why he'd been unable to escape even in death, though that hardly explained Smee. Or maybe it did. Loyalty was a funny thing.

"Pitiful."

Hook didn't turn around. He refused to give Pan the satisfaction of seeing surprise on his face again.

"I understand, though. I mean, this is a pretty good boat."

This forced Hook to turn. "Ship, you blithering idiot. The *Jolly Roger* is a ship. Best in all the oceans." He stalked toward Pan, rage building. "She can outrun the fastest of the Royal Navy, slice through the roughest waves, and do it all with a savage beauty unlike anything your *pitiful* brain can imagine."

Pan nodded, a toothy smile breaking out on his face. "That's what I thought. Just wanted to be sure."

"Of?"

He withdrew a patchwork sack from over his shoulder. "This here's a lot of pixie dust. Took forever to collect it. Didn't want to waste it on a boat—excuse me, *ship*—that wasn't worthy."

Hook sneered. "You'll never be able to sail her."

"Don't need to. I'm going to fly it."

Fly the *Jolly Roger*? Did the wicked wonders never cease?

"Where? Why?"

"Both are my business, old man."

"This ship is mine! You will tell me what you plan to do with her."

"Dead men can't own anything. It's mine now."

With a roar in his throat, Hook withdrew his sword and thrust it at Pan's chest. It dissolved into mist.

Pan laughed.

"Blast it all! Why won't you just die, ye demon?"

Pan shrugged. "Don't know, honestly. But for now, you'll have to deal with it." He jumped into the air holding the sack. "Oh, and you might want to hold on to something. Never done this before."

Hook dove beneath the main cabin's awning as Pan dusted the ship with pixie dust. The dust clung to every frayed rope and sliver of wood. The *Jolly Roger* glowed with the magic of the dust, but it remained stationary until Pan took the helm. As soon as his fingers touched the wheel, the hull lurched from the water.

Hook held on to a door to keep from rocking about. Years, his crew had been stranded in that lagoon, and now the ship rose high above the water, aiming for the sun. If only he'd known, could they have escaped?

"Hold on, Hook!" Pan called. "Don't want you falling out, do we?"

Wind caught the sails, and they fluttered to life. Dust and twigs left behind by birds seeking a place to nest clattered to the deck. The crow's nest swayed and cracked. The railing splintered from the mast and smashed onto the deck.

"Oops." Pan cackled.

"You're killing her!"

"Shut up, pirate. If there's anyone who knows how to fly, it's me."

The ship climbed slowly. The island was nothing but a spot on the massive ocean. Hook stood, gripping the bannister. They broke through the horizon, and everything went black.

No. Not all black. Stars blinked around the ship. One shot between the masts, singeing one of the sails.

Fear gripped Hook. "What is this place? Where are you taking me?"

"Calm down, old man. It's just the in-between place. Haven't thought of anything clever to call it yet. It's next on the list."

"Between where?"

"Between Neverland and the place where all Lost Boys come from." He bounced his eyebrows. "Where all pirates come from."

Home.

Could this be some kind of strange mercy from the boy? Was he taking Hook back to be at peace? Damn. Poor Smee. One more failure in Hook's time as captain.

They sailed through the night sky and into a swirling mass of stardust. Chunks of rock slammed into the sides of the ship. Hook flinched with every impact. Pan's grin only grew wider.

And then Hook blinked, and the *Jolly Roger* drifted into the choppy waters of an ocean. A proper ocean—Hook could tell by the cloudy water and gray-green foam peaking the waves. His gaze turned to Pan, not to thank him, but to pass the kind of understanding that develops between enemies, a knowledge that the fighting has ended. But Pan had disappeared below deck. He returned lugging a large black chest: Hook's personal treasures, taken from his stateroom. He watched as Pan broke the lock and tossed its contents over the main deck—gold coins, a ruby necklace, bits of leather and silverware.

"What in the name of Poseidon are you doing, boy?"

Pan winked. "Fishing."

After he finished emptying the chest, he flew to the sails and tore them to shreds. He shattered the lantern cases. Glass fell on the deck like rain. He shot one last look at Hook before flying into the light of the setting sun.

Hours passed. The sun dipped behind the horizon, and Hook started to disappear.

It began with his arms and legs. The feathery, cloudy body he'd just started to accept was falling away. Was this what it felt like to cross over? Soon, he was nothing but a voice on the wind.

Another ship, smaller than the *Jolly Roger*, but not unimpressive, pulled alongside her. There were shouts from the deck, and then she was boarded. The captain—distinguishable by his high collar and expression of superiority—kicked some of the coins. He picked one up and bit it.

"Real," he said. "All of you. Pack it up."

Hook shouted, but his voice came out as a blast of hot air with no sound. He made for the captain, to knock his treasure from the man's hands, but he only managed to graze the nose of a crewmember.

"Feels odd," the captain said.

"Really odd," one of the crew added.

"There's always a bloody ghost on these things."

"Maybe we'll get lucky. Find ourselves a lady ghost this time."

"And you'll do what, exactly, with a lady ghost, Birdie?" the captain asked.

The crew fell silent, engrossed in their treasure gathering. Only Hook saw Pan float down behind the wheel.

Fishing, he'd said.

Hook knew warning them was pointless. He was nothing. A wisp.

The ship rose out of the water and was airborne before the pirates knew what was happening. They were too frightened to jump. Too high.

"What's happening, Captain?"

"I told ye! I said! Ghosts!"

"Quiet!" the captain shouted.

The crew quieted but didn't settle. Most shot looks overboard to prove to themselves they weren't going mad.

The wheel spun, and all eyes locked on Pan.   The pirates drew their swords. Hook averted his eyes.

"Who are you?" the captain asked. "What is this magic?"

"I am Peter Pan, captain of the *Jolly Roger*."

Hook cringed.

Pan continued, "And this is a ship bound for Neverland."

It was night when they arrived in Neverland. The moon was little more than a sliver in the sky, casting just enough glow to see your face in front of your hand. One of the pirates looked in Hook's direction and yelped.

"Ghost! There be two of 'em!"

Hook looked down at himself. His ghostly form had returned. He opened his mouth to scream, to warn them, but it was too late. Pan crowed, and the Lost Boys leapt aboard the ship, slashing at anything that moved. The pirates didn't last the hour.

The next day, Hook searched the island for the Red Men camp. Rumor was the chief was the only person on the island Pan feared. Hook approached him in the open, at noon, as a show of respect. There would be no subterfuge between them.

Hook relayed the night's events. "And he's only going to do it again. Who knows what poor souls he'll lure to the island when he runs out of pirates. Sinless men. Women. Children."

The chief nodded once. "You know we do not interfere with Pan. There's a treaty to consider."

"And how long do you expect him to keep the terms? Pan is not honorable."

"Even so."

Hook argued until the sun began to set, following the chief from hut to hut, through the chief's dinner with his daughter and on into his dreams. Haunted him. All for nothing. The chief refused to do anything about Pan's evil.

But as night fell and darkness covered the island, the chief's daughter, Tiger Lily, made it clear that she did not share her father's beliefs. She snuck out of the camp once the chief was asleep. Hook followed.

She climbed the hill overlooking the widest arc of the lagoon. Using a feathered cape as a kind of parachute, she drifted onto the deck of the *Jolly Roger*. She searched below deck until she found one of the last barrels of gunpowder. Working quickly, she planted one end of a long line of thread in the barrel. Then she set the other end on fire.

With Hook watching from the hill, Tiger Lily leapt into the lagoon as the *Jolly Roger* exploded in flames.

From the diary of Wendy Moira Angela Darling

What an idiot I am.

I left Neverland. I forced Peter to take my brothers and me home.

So why then, Diary, am I back again?

He came for me the night before I was to be sent to Paris for school. Though I wasn't keen on the idea of a boarding school, I was anxious to get away from that house and (forgive me) my brothers. It's been a year, and John still isn't speaking. Michael clings to Mother's skirts as though letting go will rip the very breath from his lungs.

I wanted to forget Peter, and I'd very nearly succeeded.

Who am I kidding? I will never forget him.

This time, the poor boy sacrificed to Pan's games was one I hadn't met before. His name was Charlie. Peter hated him for no other reason than that the boys looked up to him.

How could they not? He was kind and clever (I dare say cleverer than Pan) and not to mention, handsome. Charlie took to the gallows as nobly as Sydney Carton, from Mother's favorite Dickens novel. When the light left his eyes, and his body ceased to move, I couldn't bring myself to finish my abridged version of Romeo and Juliet. The boys and I cried while Pan looked on *in disgust. And in that moment, I wondered how I could have ever loved a boy like him.*

Then.

I hate that word.

Then, with a few whispered words and his gentle, sweet breath on my face before he kissed me, I was Pan's once more.

Don't think me stupid. It was a temporary lapse, though I worry that if left unchecked, they'll continue, and I'll be Pan's companion in murder for the rest of my days.

There's only one way to end all this. Though I can't bring myself to commit the thought to paper, I know what I have to do. God, give me strength and a sharp blade.

Chapter Twenty-Five

"Liz and I'd just had a fight," Slightly began. "A row bigger than any of the others."

Madge listened, keeping thoughts of Jane floating through her mind. What happened if she forgot her mother the way Slightly forgot his?

Slightly continued, "She had her heart set on marrying this buffoon. Mort. What the hell kind of a name is Mort? Anyway, I'd seen what he did to girls who pissed him off. George's sister, Milly, had her face beaten in for not lifting her skirts when he told her to. My dad had gone away to work, somewhere on the other side of the country, so I was the man of the house. I forbade her to see him, and she went completely mental.

"So one night, I'm holed up in the attic, looking through some of my dad's things. I had it in my head to tie Liz to a chair until she saw reason. I had everything ready: rope, a clean gag for her mouth. Then Pan showed up."

"And?"

"And nothing. I left."

"Just like that?"

"He was very convincing." Slightly smirked. "'Course, you know all about that."

Madge's cheeks warmed. "I wanted to know about my family."

"We all had our reasons."

The forest quieted as they trudged toward the others. Once Pan's fireball was in sight, Slightly paused. "Probably best if you keep calling me Slightly."

"But it's not your name."

"It's my name here. And it's not that bad of a name, is it? I'm the only one with my own name, you know. Pan chose everyone else's once they forgot the ones they were born with. I discovered mine on the tag of a laundry bag that'd gotten mixed into my things."

"But..."

"Look, Madge, I'm not stupid enough to believe my family is still alive out there somewhere. They're long dead, which means I have nothing waiting for me outside of Neverland. I'm glad I remember them, but that's all it is."

"But you didn't remember them. Until a minute ago, you had no idea where you came from."

"Maybe that's the magic of Neverland. This place takes care of lost kids. Sometimes, forgetting is best."

Madge frowned. "Did my mother forget me? Is that why she never came back?"

Slightly shook his head. "Jane was different. All you Darlings are different."

She raked her nails over her face. That was all anyone could say to her. So far, all being different had done was land her in Hell. "I don't buy it."

"What?"

"None of it."

"Yeah. I figured you wouldn't." He shook his head. "Just don't do anything dumb, okay?"

"No promises."

Slaughtered. More than half of her tribe torn to pieces by Pan and his band of demons. Tiger Lily cradled the covered head of Elder, her mentor and friend, as the remaining women anointed his body with sweet-smelling oils and petals. She should have stopped Pan. She should have gotten back to her people sooner, fought harder. *Something.* Instead, she'd been chasing the possibility of freedom from tyranny. She should have known Pan wouldn't be killed so easily.

The girl was weak, and Tiger Lily shouldn't have been so stupid as to believe otherwise. The ghost convinced her, but in the end, the ghost was still a pirate. Pirates were not to be trusted.

Neverbirds gathered overhead, flying in a wide circle over the dead, their dirge low and sorrowful. As Elder was lowered into the ground, Tiger Lily cut her palm and placed it against his figure on the wall.

"Goodbye, old friend," she said. "Your death will not be in vain."

Soon the dirge of the Neverbirds was drowned by the song of her phoenix. It rained sparks over the graves, blessing the dead with its sacred dance of new life.

Tiger Lily ran to her hut and tied the door closed. "Hook!"

He appeared moments later. "I am not to be summoned like a mutt."

"And yet, you come when called."

"Not to be insulted."

"You knew Pan was coming."

Hook paused. "I… suspected. He doesn't abide insult."

"I would do more than insult him."

"Yes. We both know how badly you wish to skewer the blaggard's heart. I would gladly watch as you roasted it over a pit and fed it to his mongrels. We also know it's not that simple."

Tiger Lily slammed her fist into the side of the hut. "Tell me what you know, pirate. You owe me. Or have you forgotten the death at sea I granted your precious *Jolly Roger*?"

"How could I forget?" he said coolly. "I've told you. Pan's aging. He thinks it's because his boys are growing older, but I suspect differently. The island and Pan are linked on a kind of spiritual level, but lately, it has seemed as though the island is trying to break that connection."

"How do you mean?"

"Look up."

She rolled her eyes. "What does the sun have to do with anything?"

"Pan's been to war today. Shouldn't the skies be black? Where's the lightning? The celebratory thunder?"

Tiger Lily considered Hook. He might have been right. He might have been insane. She couldn't imagine what being dead could do to a person's mind.

"What's your point?" she asked.

"We have to get him off the island."

"And how do you plan to do that?"

"The girl."

Tiger Lily scowled. "Weakling."

"I think she'll surprise us."

"How do you figure that?"

His face darkened to the color of smoke. "I've seen her type before. Long time ago."

She turned away from him. How many more people would die while she attempted the impossible? Pan was immortal, and it was time to accept it. Perhaps her father had been right all along. "I'll have no part in your riddles, Hook. Leave me and my people to mourn in peace."

"On one condition."

She sighed. "Pirate to the end."

"When I give the word, meet me at the lagoon."

She glanced over her shoulder. "Why?"

But Hook was gone.

Chapter Twenty-Six

THE NIGHT WAS MERCIFULLY LONG and still, and Madge slept. She found the boys' snores comforting. When they slept, they weren't warriors. They were just boys.   She woke several times in the night, wondering where and if Pan slept—if he watched her from some hiding place in the upper reaches of the tree. But then exhaustion won, and she was asleep again, dreaming of the Red Men.

The morning came on bright and angry. A hatch somewhere was left open, and the sun pounded through onto Madge's face. She opened her eyes to see Pan's face an inch from her own. His smile was all teeth, and his eyes sparkled.

He kissed her forehead. "Rise and shine, Mother. It's time."

All of the boys were still sleeping, except for Slightly. Out of the corner of her eye, she saw him peer up at her from beneath a ratty blanket.

"Time for what?"

"Meet me outside in five minutes." He winked. "Or I'll have to come in after you."

"'Kay."

Pan bounded through the tunnel, crowing.

Two days-ish of no shower had made Madge's hair gritty and tangled. She ripped a bit of root from above her bunk and twisted it around her hair to keep it back. Slightly still watched her. She met his gaze, and he turned over in bed.

She stared at Slightly's back. "What's your problem?"

He didn't answer.

As she sipped from a wooden cup of water left by her bunk, she eyed the rest of the Lost Boys. She caught most of their glances—beady little raccoon eyes—before they all turned away like they were ashamed of her.

"Bye, then." She crawled into the tunnel.

Pan waited for her by the mouth, usually hidden behind a hollow rock. "This way." He marched into the jungle, keeping away from their usual path to the feast table.

"What? No flying?"

"Wouldn't be fair if I flew, now, would it?"

"Where are we going?"

Silence. He easily jumped over a waist-high log that Madge scraped her legs climbing.

"Hey!" Madge scrambled to keep up. This was ridiculous. "I'm not going any further until you give me something."

He didn't stop. "What do you want?"

So much for a standoff. She had to run to keep up. "Why am I here?"

"You asked to find your mother."

"And I found her. I want to go home now."

He laughed. "Why would you want to go home when you could be here? What does that pathetic little town have that Neverland doesn't?"

"A little sanity, maybe?"

"You just haven't fully experienced it yet."

"I've experienced enough." Madge stopped. "Take me home. Now."

Pan stroked the hilt of his sword.

A chill passed through Madge's body.

"Tell you what, Madge. I'll make a deal with you."

She stiffened.

"I planned on taking you on a little morning hunt. If you're going to be here, you're going to earn your keep. If you're so intent on leaving, I'll let you, but only if you kill us a boar for the table first."

"And I'm supposed to just trust you'll keep your word?"

"I always do."

"You promised me my mother."

"You found her, didn't you?"

"Not with your help!"

"Who says?"

She paused, gnawing her lip.

Pan shrugged. "We both know you don't have a choice, so you might as well be a good sport about it."

He was right. She wondered how hard she could throw a punch at his cocky grin. "You expect me to kill the thing with my bare hands?"

"That's my girl." Pan dove behind a dead-looking tree and returned with two spears. The pointed ends were tied to knotty, twisted sticks with strips of twine.

He handed one of them to Madge. It wasn't as heavy as she thought it would be. Awkward to handle, though, like she was more likely to spear the ground than anything that moved. Pan took off running too fast for her to follow.

"There's no way in hell I'm winning this," she muttered. She'd have to be clever, but how clever could she be against a boy who could manipulate the time of day to suit his mood?

The jungle trees seemed to close in on her like green walls. She found a narrow path made of bent reeds and followed it. About ten feet along, she stopped. Changed her mind. Pan probably put the path there to throw her off, maybe send her off a cliff somewhere.

Madge veered right, holding the spear out in front of her. It was helpful in bashing tough weeds and vines out of the way. As she ventured further, the ground grew soft and muddy. Her shoes sank in about an inch with each step. All manner of scary scenarios ran through her mind—death traps, sinkholes, quicksand, Snowball looking for someone to play with.

As though on cue, a snorting, growling sound erupted from behind her. She turned faster than she could drag the spear, and it scraped the side of a tree, getting caught in the fungus-y bark. She cursed, yanking the thing free. To her right, she spotted something big and brown running away. Madge wasn't sure what a boar looked like. Big and piggish, she imagined, and probably brown. Could it really be this easy?

She took off after the thing, which was surprisingly quick. The tail flew in erratic patterns as though not totally attached to the animal. She hurdled fallen trees and tangles of grass that reached up to wrap around her ankles. Her knees quivered, buckling as she landed sideways over an abandoned pile of coconut shells. But she never lost sight of her goal. It was dangerous to hold on to hope that she might win, but she couldn't help it. She was so close.

The thing squealed as it ran between trees that packed closer together the deeper into the jungle she chased it. For an instant, it got caught under a low limb and scampered free just as Madge reached stabbing distance.

So close.

Her vision tunneled, and the jungle seemed to fall away. Her prey was never more than six or seven feet ahead of her. Somewhere, a branch cracked, and the boar paused. Madge didn't hesitate. In three steps, she was on it and brought the spear down between its shoulder blades. It cried out—

Cried out?

Madge bent over, hands on her knees, sucking in deep breaths. Her pulse pounded in her temples as her vision returned to normal. The trees above rustled as Pan broke the canopy and settled in front of her. She didn't like the way he was smiling.

"Looks like you won."

She nodded once. "Yeah. Now you're going to take me home, right?"

"It wasn't that difficult for you, though, was it? I mean, the thing might as well have been, I don't know, a child, with how fast it was running."

Madge frowned. "I got lucky, I guess."

He snorted. "Maybe."

Footsteps echoed in the distance. Madge crouched, preparing for some kind of attack. Another boar stuffed its snout between a couple of bramble bushes.

"Guess you didn't even get to yours." Madge relaxed.

"I wasn't trying." He turned to the boar. "Game's over, Jinx."

The boar rose onto its hind legs and then peeled the skin off its face and back. It fell in a heap at the feet of a Lost Boy—a boar in disguise.

Her gaze flew between the false boar and the one with her spear sticking out of its side. How could she not have seen it? She replayed the chase in her mind, searching for any small detail that should have given it away, but came up with nothing. It was like something evil had taken over, disguising the boy's obviously human legs and arms. Revulsion racked her body. She was a murderer. "You tricked me."

"Not a trick," Pan said. "A game."

Madge couldn't move. Couldn't breathe. She didn't dare turn to look at the boy lying dead behind her.

Jinx knelt at the "boar's" head. "Dead."

Pan grinned. "Mother's a good shot."

Tears pricked her eyes. Her hands shook, and her knees gave. "I didn't know…"

"Least he went quick," Jinx said.

Grief warmed until it was a fiery rage. Madge stood, quicker than she thought possible, and stole the spear from Pan's hand. She aimed the sharp end at his jugular, so close it pricked the skin. "You tricked me into killing that boy. Why? What has he ever done to you?"

Pan was unmoved. "Nothing. He hasn't done anything to you either, yet you condemned him to die."

"I didn't."

"You chose him. Jinxy here too."

"No, I—"

"Yes, you didn't know. But that's the point of it. That's what makes it *fun*."

A single drop of ruby blood slid down Pan's throat. Madge wanted him to bleed more. "How could this possibly be fun?"

He shrugged. "Watching you consider killing me is pretty amusing."

She barely flinched. It was enough.

The spear was gone, and Pan's hands gripped hers so hard she thought they might break. "I did trick you. I admit that. But it was for your own good. See, if you go back home now, you'll carry Curly's blood on you for the rest of your life. You'll be a murderer. If you stay here, you'll just be another lost boy."

"Girl," Jinx said.

"The point is, Madge, you belong here now. With me." Pan nudged Jinx's shoulder in a brotherly way. It was sickening how Jinx so obviously craved the attention. "With us."

She wanted to fight him, to say he was wrong. But she blinked first. He was right. Madge was a murderer. Her shoulders fell inward, and she wanted to just keep folding until she was nothing but a square on the ground to be trampled. She was nothing. Less than nothing.

"Aw, Madge." Pan released her hands and pulled her into a crushing embrace. "It's not in vain, you know. The boys were going to die anyway."

Jinx's ears perked up at the plural.

Pan continued, "I owe some nice fish ladies double."

The walk to the shore was mostly quiet. Tootles carried Curly in his arms, wrapped in a blanket, but Curly's mop of springy black hair was still visible. Jinx stared ahead, arms tight at his sides. Even the birds sat in somber solidarity in the tallest branches of the thickest trees. Pan whistled a tuneless melody.

Slightly walked just behind Madge. His fingers occasionally grazed hers as they walked.

"Looks like you and Slightly are getting cozy," Pan said.

Slightly's head turned a millimeter.

"Is that bad?" Madge asked.

"No, no. Of course not." Pan slipped his arm through hers. "If you're going to be at home here, I want you to be comfortable with my men."

Jealousy, she thought. *That's the last thing I need.*

Soon, she smelled salt water on the breeze. Jinx was visibly tense—jaw clenching, steps robotic—but continued on. This was what blind faith in their leader had brought them, to be considered expendable for the sake of a boat. But it wasn't faith, was it? It was love. Slightly had left his family after being brushed off. How many of these boys' stories were the same? Madge would've bet all of them. They really were lost boys, drawn to Pan by his offers of companionship and brotherhood. And wasn't that why she left her home too? For answers to the million whys and whens of her family?

"They love you," she said.

"And I them."

"Sick way of showing it."

Pan stopped, holding her back from the group as they continued toward the shore. He met her gaze. Gone was the merry twinkle, replaced by ice pools. "I've given them my life. I helped create this world for them. For us. For kids who get thrown away over a new baby or a drab future or just because their parents decide, out of the blue, their lives would be better with one less mouth to feed. I give these boys adventure! I give them *life*." They continued to walk, keeping their distance. "Is it not also my right to take it away?"

"No." Madge ripped her arm from his hold. "It isn't."

Pan's smile returned, haughty and sharp. "Just wait. You'll see it my way soon."

"I won't."

"You will. Just like Wendy did."

Her voice caught.

"Look alive, Darling. We're here."

The trees cleared, and she was back on the beach. The boys gathered in a half-circle around Curly and Jinx. Jinx stood defiant, face forward, shoulders back, while Tootles's legs were turned in at the knees, eyes cast downward at his fallen friend.

"Gonna pee himself," Nibs muttered.

Madge pulled away from Pan's side. He didn't seem to care. She positioned herself in front of Jinx, blocking his view of the waves lapping at the shore like hungry tongues.

"Look at me," she said. "You can run. Run and I'll find you, and I'll take you away from here."

Slightly sucked in a breath. Shook his head.

She ignored him.

"Can't run," Jinx muttered.

"Why?"

"Pan."

"I can protect you." She only half believed it.

Nibs snickered.

"Shut it," she snapped. She turned back to Jinx. "Run."

But he didn't run.

Pan whistled three high notes followed by a low tone that sounded like a ship's horn.

"Mother," Jinx said, "will you tell us a story?"

The surface of the water calmed as a dozen mermaids emerged. The closest wore a look of contempt, gills prickling like the back of an angry cat. "How dare you summon us with the call of our people!"

"Got your attention, didn't it?" Pan gestured to the boys. "I have payment."

Tears collected in the corners of Madge's eyes. She brought her face close to the boys'. "Once upon a time, there were two boys. Their names were Curly and Jinx."

"What about Tootles?" Tootles asked.

Slightly elbowed him in the gut.

The mermaid bared pointed teeth. "I demanded double."

"Can you fish-people count? One, two. Double."

"They are small, and that one is already dead."

Madge continued, "And they may have been small, but they had big, brave hearts. They lived in a magical land where they went on lots of adventures."

Pan scoffed. "There are two of them. That was the deal. Where's my ship?"

Scowling, the mermaid pointed toward a small island a mile or so offshore. As she pointed, waves rolled in from the east and nudged an anchored ship into the open—three masts, billowing white sails, and a foreign flag waving defiantly from the crow's nest.

"Perfect," he said.

"And on these adventures," Madge said, "Curly and Jinx performed heroic deeds. They slew evil witches and rescued damsels. They climbed to the tallest room of the tallest tower and recovered a golden egg that hatched into a dragon. They named him—"

"Martin," Jinx interjected.

"Martin was a white dragon. He flew high in the sky until he was just another cloud."

"Payment," the mermaid said. "Now."

Madge heard the crunch of Pan's feet in the sand. She held Jinx's hand as she finished the story. "And after all those adventures, the boys were tired. They lay down in the sand of their favorite beach, and sleep fell over them like a wave, and they dreamed only the best dreams."

"The end," Jinx said.

"Well done, Mother." Pan took Jinx's hand. He didn't struggle. Curly was tossed over Pan's shoulder like an animal.

Madge's breath came in short bursts. Her eyes burned, and her chest ached. She could free Jinx herself. Drag him from the beach. But she knew he'd only come back.

Pan led them to the shore, where water crested over Jinx's feet. "Off you go."

Jinx walked until the water was too deep to walk. Pan tossed Curly into the waves. The mermaids disappeared beneath the surface, and with barely a ripple, the boys were dragged under.

Pan leaped into the air and crowed, beating on his chest. He saluted the remaining boys, who saluted in return. He somersaulted into a breeze and rode it toward his ship.

Madge watched the water, willing the boys to come up. To breathe. To laugh because it was all a big joke. Slightly joined her, his hand so close to hers she could feel its heat.

"I'm going to kill Pan," she said.

Slightly nodded. "How can I help?"

From the diary of Wendy Moira Angela Darling;

He knew my plan before I did. I was foolish to think I could do anything on this godforsaken island without Peter knowing.

It's that shadow of his. Pan's second eyes.

Foolish of me to think I could kill Peter with a knife. Foolish of me to think I could kill him at all.

"Silly girl," he said, smacking the pitiful blade from my hand.

"I'm not silly, nor am I a girl. I'm a woman."

"If that were true, you wouldn't be here. Neverland can't hold men or women. It would die."

"I hope it does."

And when I said it, something passed over his face that made him look, for the first time, really, properly human.

"I forgive you, Wendy," he said. "For everything."

He forgives me? The audacity! I would've struck him if he hadn't leapt into the air to twirl about my head and pull my hair.

"Face it. Your heart belongs here. It will always be here. You leave, but your heart stays. You know it, and that's why you're angry."

As he brought me back to London, I vowed never to return. A vow I intend to keep at all costs.

It's true. My heart does belong to Neverland. But who needs a heart?

Chapter Twenty-Seven

Once upon a time...

SOMETHING WAS WRONG WITH JANE. Peter had noticed it the first time one morning about a month ago. She'd puked up an entire meal of perfectly good saber and star fruit stew only to take his after. Always hungry. Always sick. Jane was spending a lot of time at the piss pit too. Her shit stank worse than Tootles's, and the stench took forever to dissipate.

The constant complaining. She fell behind during all the best games, claiming she was too tired, or her back ached. To top it off, Jane was getting fat. Not Tootles fat, but still pudgy around the middle. Gone were the hard hipbones Pan likened to knives and the graceful inward slope of her belly.

"Bloated," she'd said. "Too many potatoes."

Pan had half a mind to send Jane back to Wendy, regardless of what that'd do to his plans to destroy her. But then he'd remember Wendy's final words to him—*you meant nothing to me*—and renewed energy took root in his gut. Besides, even fat, Jane wasn't terrible to look at. He particularly liked her collarbone, how it looked like someone had scooped the flesh from either side of her neck. Sometimes, he wanted to bite it.

Today, Pan decided he wanted snow. The summer had been hard on him—that blasted sun, always blazing hotter than he intended. So far, he'd only been able to make it snow on Snowball's part of the island. Poor thing didn't have enough room to play. Pan stood on a hill overlooking the densest part of the jungle, where most of the clouds liked to gather. He thought cold thoughts. *Snowflakes. The deepest, darkest part of the ocean. Mermaid skin. Ice.* Soon, the clouds thickened to puffy, gray marshmallows, fat with snow ready to fall.   He smiled and continued imagining.

"Peter?"

His smile evaporated. If he ignored her, she'd go away. *Dirt from deep in the ground. Morning dew on the grass.*

Jane waddled in front of him, blocking his view of the jungle. When had she gotten so big? Her belly curved like a ball. His cold thoughts fizzled along with the clouds.

"What do you want?"

The corners of her mouth pulled down, almost forming a V on her chin. "We need to talk."

"So talk."

"No. You talk. You've been ignoring *this* since I started showing." She pointed to her belly. "We have to do something."

"Ignoring what? That you're getting fat? I thought it'd be kinder not to mention it."

"I'm not getting fat!" Tears streamed down her face. *God, the friggin' tears.* "I'm pregnant!"

He laughed. "Nonsense. Pigs get pregnant. Not people."

"You can't be serious."

He shrugged. At first, he'd liked Jane because she wasn't a puzzle. She hadn't stayed that way.

Jane snatched his hand and held it against her stomach. She'd gotten surprisingly strong and held his hand there until a weird, fluttering something nudged his palm. He squinted, as though limiting his vision could help him feel better. Another nudge. He hadn't imagined it.

No.

"How?" he asked.

Instead of an answer, it only brought more sobs, stronger and more guttural than before. He couldn't deal with her like this, couldn't deal with anyone like this. He made a decision. Jane was going back to Wendy.

Chapter Twenty-Eight

IT WAS A SHIP, ALL right, but it wasn't the *Jolly Roger*. Even though he was a filthy, rotten pirate who deserved everything he got, Captain Hook, at least, had had taste. There were tears in the main sail and chunks missing out of the starboard side of the ship. It'd been in a fight, and Pan only regretted he hadn't been there to see it. There was a simple carving at the bow of a woman with large breasts and fins—a poor representation of a mermaid. Pan chuckled, thinking of the sailors who'd once populated this ship, thinking of their faces falling and their balls shrinking as they realized the object of their fantasy was more suited to their nightmares.

Cursed were the ships that wandered into Neverland.

Pan inspected the wheel, frowning. It looked like a normal wheel—considering his limited familiarity with the subject of ship mechanics—and turned like a normal wheel.

While he was content to let the occasional ship invade the shores of Neverland—the boys were always in need of new game to hunt—Pan had spent an exhausting amount of time trying to figure out why. Each dead end in his investigation led to a solid week of storms. He'd been the heart of Neverland for a long, long time. In all that time, no one had ever found his way to the island except by ship or by his personal invitation.

Not that he was complaining. Pan was a leader, and a leader wasn't a leader without followers or things to lead toward. He just wanted to *know*.

It'd take a lot of fairy dust to cover the ship if he wanted to get it to the Other World, more than he had. The fairy-mating season was almost over, and any chance of getting what he needed—regardless of his weather meddling—was shrinking by the day.

He should bring Madge. Get her mind off the morning's unpleasantness. Pan wasn't so self-absorbed as to not notice she was upset. But she did so *well*. A natural. Like Wendy.

"But she doesn't love me," he said.

His shadow leaned against the shadow of a support beam and shrugged.

Pan didn't expect the shadow to answer. He wasn't *crazy*. When he'd first arrived in Neverland, alone, lost, it was Tiger Lily's grandmother who'd showed him how to separate his shadow from himself—to create a friend, or at least, someone to talk to.

"Wendy loved me so easily. Everything about her was easy. It doesn't make sense. Why is Madge such a…" He rubbed his chin, searching for the right word to describe just how difficult she was. His fingers brushed a new patch of hair.

He froze, running his fingertips over the patch. Over and over. It was like the grass that surrounded the tree house—prickly. Unsheathing his dagger, Pan ran for the nearest reflective surface—a window—and dragged the blade along his chin until his skin was smooth. A drop of blood fell down his neck.

It isn't fair, he thought. "I don't want to grow up."

The shadow drifted upward until its head was surrounded by the shadow of a rope, cast from across the ship. A halo.

Pan nodded. "You're right. I need to bring youth to the island. These boys are growing up and killing the spirit of Neverland. As its protector, I can't let it stand."

He patted the wheel and gave it a hard spin, which sloshed water up the sides. "Slightly will be first."

And then Madge will have room in her heart to love me, and she'll be my mother, and we'll take this ship to the Other World and bring her more sons, and all will be well.

Nibs rolled a stitched leather ball toward the wall. When it didn't come back, he pouted before crawling to retrieve it.

"Play with me," he said to Madge.

She folded Jinx's blanket and tucked it beside her pillow. "I don't feel like playing."

"Aw, you're no fun. Slightly?"

Slightly shook his head.

Nibs turned to Tootles, but he'd already snatched up the ball and heaved it at Nibs's face. Madge flinched at the audible crack. Blood dripped from his nose.

"My nose!"

"That's what you get for drippin' your boogers all over the place. Crybaby."

Nibs stood. His nose was crooked, and blood bubbled when he spoke. "I wasn't crying."

"Crybaby."

"Asshole!"

"Ooo. Big words for such a small"—Tootles jabbed his shoulder—"boy."

Madge jumped from her bunk and smashed a bunch of somewhat clean leaves against Nibs' nose. Unbelievable, the way these boys went at each other when they'd just watched their fearless leader sacrifice their friends for a boat.

Once the bleeding slowed, Madge grabbed his nose. "This is gonna hurt."

He nodded.

She yanked—never mind that she'd only ever seen this done on television—and Nibs howled. It looked at least somewhat normal now.

She turned to Tootles, cross-legged on Curly's bunk. "If you're trying to make us believe you don't care about what just happened, save it. We all know."

"I don't—"

"Are you back-talking Mother?" Slightly snapped.

Tootles shook his head.

Madge sneered. "Don't call me that."

Slightly shrugged.

Sighing, she climbed back into her bunk. She dug through her backpack and found a piece of stale gum, still in the wrapper. She tossed it to Nibs, who buried it somewhere in his bunk. The food and knife were gone from her bag, but the book was still there. She fingered the spine, wondering if there was anything of use in the pages. She knew it was Grandma Wendy's diary. The first pages were full of praise and love for Pan. It was disgusting.

Slightly climbed in next to her. "It's not going to be easy."

"Never said it would be."

"I mean really, really not easy."

"Chickening out?"

He sighed. "No. I'm just saying that it's probably going to get us killed. You haven't been here long enough to see the kind of hold he has on this place."

Her gaze drifted to Tootles and Nibs, passing the leather ball back and forth. "I see plenty."

"Then you have a plan?"

"Nope."

"Well, I certainly feel better."

"I'll figure it out."

Slightly patted her leg. "Figure it out soon, or plan on not figuring it out at all."

The hatch opened, and Pan fell through, landing on his feet in front of Slightly and Madge. There was a spot of dried blood on his neck. "I have an announcement." His eyes locked on Slightly.

"Me first," Madge said.

Pan frowned.

"I've decided something."

Slightly raised an eyebrow.

Pan looked from Slightly to Madge. "Oh?"

She nodded. "Mhmm. We haven't spent any real time together. If I'm going to be expected to live here now, I want to feel like this is really my home. Get to know the place. Get to know you."

Pan grinned, and his voice lost a touch of its bravado. "So you've seen reason?" He sounded almost pleading.

She shrugged, hoping her contempt didn't show through.

Pan beat his chest and crowed. The walls of the tree vibrated and rained dirt.

Nibs whistled. "Mother's staying!"

Pan leaped into the air, twirling, somersaulting, and parrying an invisible foe.

Slightly leaned in and whispered, "What are you doing?"

Madge spied his pocketknife sticking out of his shorts. She snatched it. "Figuring it out."

"Let's start now," Pan called from the branches.

"Yes," Madge said through a clenched smile. "Let's."

She blinked, and she was in the air. Gold dust fell in her eyes, and it was hard to see. When the dust cleared, she was greeted by a blue, cloudless sky, and the tree house was a shrinking twig. A current blew through, and with Pan's guidance, they rode it like a roller coaster. Neverbirds joined behind, falling into a V. One squawked in her ear, and Madge laughed in spite of herself.

Pan pulled her higher where the wind was faster and colder. "You could do this every day."

"What if it rains?"

He laughed. "Silly girl. It never rains unless I command it. I control the day and night. The seasons. The wind." A gust nearly knocked her hand out of his. "I want to share it with you."

A chill passed through her, and her lips went numb. "I'm freezing."

"Oh. Right. Sorry."

They dipped downward toward the ocean. There was no sign of the green-haired child-eaters, but Madge knew they were there. The air warmed, and her shivers slowed.

"Where are we going?"

Pan pointed, and in the distance she spotted a small stone island. It wasn't until they got closer that she saw it was in the shape of a skull. His ship sat, ghostlike, next to it. Skull Rock, he'd called it.

"What's at Skull Rock?"

His eyes twinkled. "A surprise."

They landed on a boulder shaped like a cracked tooth. The entire island was about the size of the ship, spotted with weeds and algae sloshed up from the ocean. A rotting fish, picked clean of its flesh except for the head, glistened in the sunlight.

"Do you remember when you first got here, and I showed you the fairies?"

Madge nodded.

"Tonight is the last night they make dust before hibernation. It'll happen up there." He pointed to the top of the skull. "Under the open sky."

"It's summer."

"Spring, actually." A small smile crept over his face. "But the fairies have never been to the island. They follow their own instincts."

Madge craned her neck up. "We'll fly up there?"

He nodded, reaching into a leather satchel tied to his belt. He withdrew a handful of gold dust and threw it over her.

Her breath caught as she was launched up about a foot.

"Pixie dust. Everyone on this island needs it to fly."

"Even you?"

He frowned. "Unfortunately."

Grabbing her hand, he guided her up the side of Skull Rock until they rested on the crown. Her stomach growled.

"Hungry?" he asked.

"Apparently."

He winked and placed his hand on the rock. His face turned pink and purple with effort until finally, a green vine snaked upward, and white blooms turned red and round and plump. They were the sweet tomatoes from her first feast.

"Remembered. You. Liked these," he said, out of breath.

She nodded, confused. She didn't think he'd been paying attention to her at all.

"Eat."

Madge didn't wait to be told twice. She plucked a tomato from the vine and popped it whole into her mouth. Juice washed over her tongue, and she moaned with pleasure. She ate three more before looking up. He was watching her like a child watches zoo animals—with fascination and a little fear.

"More?"

"No." She shrank, ashamed. Two boys had died today, and she was gorging herself on magic fruit.

Pan ignored her, growing another, this time with silver blooms that turned yellow and round and plump. He plucked one and handed it to her.

Covering her mouth with her hand, she took a modest bite. It tasted like a chocolate-covered banana. "It's good."

"Good." He smiled. "Good."

The smile threw her, not because it was menacing—she'd seen a dozen of those—but because it looked... sincere. *Soft, upturned lips and no sharpness in his eyes.* His hands fidgeted in his lap, and his gaze darted around, pausing on Madge just long enough to catch her eye, then leaving again. Pan was nervous.

Madge didn't know whether to be terrified or laugh. "So when does this thing happen?"

"Nightfall."

"I'm surprised you haven't forced the sun down yet."

He chuckled. "Like I said, the fairies do their own thing."

Slightly's knife felt heavy against her thigh. She couldn't forget why she was here. To learn.

"Seems you know everything about everything, including me."

He blushed.

The smallest of human acts. She ignored it. "But I don't know anything about you."

"I'm Peter Pan," he said, as though that was enough.

She raised an eyebrow. "And?"

He shrugged and drew on the ground with a bit of juice from a yellow tomato. "What do you want to know?"

"Is that your real name?"

"Is now."

"And before?"

"Don't really remember before."

"How'd you get here?"

"Flew."

"How?"

He scowled. "Why does everything have to have a *why* or *how*? Why can't it just be?"

"Because that's not how the world works."

"It's how my world works." Pan waved a stiff hand, and the sun disappeared behind the horizon as a pair of moons rose.

Frustrated, Madge peeled the skin from one of the red tomatoes. She was getting nothing. All she learned was what she already knew. Pan only cared about himself. She looked up to ask him to take her back to the tree house, and his lips met hers. They were clumsy and insistent. His fingers dug into her shoulders, and she tried to shove him away, but he was stronger. He pushed her onto her back, and she shoved her knee up and into his stomach. He howled in her face, releasing her shoulders to clutch his middle. Tears stung her eyes as she hobbled backward on her butt and elbows.

He stood in the center of the moonlight. Madge noticed a bulge in the front of his tunic. He pushed down on it, whimpering, "No, no, no."

Madge's heart hammered, and her hands felt clammy. She'd slip if she tried to climb down now. Would she be able to fly?

With a mournful howl, he launched into the air and disappeared into the night.

From the diary of Wendy Moira Angela Darling

I had a dream about Peter tonight. There was blood and feathers and that raucous laughter I delighted in as a girl. George says it's only a nightmare, but I know what it means.

Peter's coming for Jane.

I tried to run away, but all I've done is delay the inevitable. I have two choices. Deny Peter and watch as he snatches my only child by force, or allow her to accompany him, just this once. Appease him, so that he'll return her to me whole and unharmed.

George will never forgive me, but it's the only way.

A thought occurs to me, and I'm almost too terrified to even consider—

What if she decides to love him?

Chapter Twenty-Nine

I T WAS OBVIOUS PAN WASN'T coming back, but Madge couldn't stop staring at the sky for a sign of him. He'd kissed her and hated that he'd kissed her. Hated what it did to him.

Madge had only kissed one boy before: Jared Perkins from homeroom. He'd followed her to the girl's bathroom, said he liked her, and kissed her. Then he'd pulled down his pants and showed her his little-boy erection. He'd expected her to reciprocate, and she would have, if a bunch of girls hadn't come in and dragged him out by the ankles. Afterward, when her grandmother found out, they'd had a *talk*. Madge knew something like that only happened to boys when they were becoming men.

Pan was growing up.

"Are you all right, dear?" Hook hovered just above the ground behind her. His ghost-form reflected the moonlight in a way that made him glow.

"Is it true?" she asked. "Pan's growing up?"

He nodded. "Aye. Pan is a boy of magic, but even boys of magic cannot control the cranks of Father Time."

"That's why he brings the boys here. Kills them. To slow the clock."

"Not a bad theory, I'll admit. It would certainly explain his sudden taste for life on the sea."

Madge's breath came faster, shallower. How could she have allowed herself to think, even for a second, that he was anything but evil? "The boat. He's going to use it to abduct dozens of kids and bring them back here."

"Aye."

"Captain!" a voice called from below.

Hook shook his head. "A moment, if you please, Smee."

Madge peered over the edge and saw Smee's ghost, flickering in and out of the light as he bobbed in a small rowboat. "You came in a boat?"

"Ah, the irony of it all. Ghosts—even the ghosts of the sea-faring type such as myself—cannot cross water unassisted. An irony, if you'll pardon the assumption, which seems to work out in your favor."

She returned her gaze to the sky. "What do I do?"

"Even with the boys here, time can only be slowed while Pan is in Neverland. Once he crosses into your world, time proceeds as usual."

Realization dawned. "I have to trap him there."

"Easier said than done, dear Madge. As I'm sure you've noticed, our young demon can fly."

"With pixie dust," she said, remembering the sack on his belt. "I think I've got an idea."

"Splendid. Now, let's get you off this thing before the tide comes in. When Pan's having one of his tantrums, it can be rather nasty."

"Nothing the captain of the *Jolly Roger* can't handle!" Smee called from below.

Hook smirked. "Bless his poor, damned soul. He tries so hard."

She arrived at the tree house only to be greeted by silence. She opened the hatch. The air inside felt heavy and electric with Wrong. She slid through the opening and onto a branch, which lowered her to the ground. The eyes of the remaining Lost Boys—and Pan—fixed on her.

"Glad you made it home safely, Mother," Pan said.

"Yeah." Madge offered a brief smile. "No sweat."

He sat in his horned throne while the boys kneeled around him. Slightly stood, sequestered in a corner.

"As I was saying," Pan said, "Slightly has been chosen to serve Neverland."

Slightly straightened, arms stiff at his sides. His mouth pinched, and his eyes were slits, like he was trying not to cry.

"No." Madge's voice cracked. "Not like Curly and Jinx served Neverland?"

"As I wanted to explain to you earlier before..." Pan paused. "Slightly has reached the end of his time."

"Gonna hang him," Tootles mumbled.

"Hang him?" Tears burned her eyes, but she blinked them back. Pan would not get to her. She had to keep some measure of control if there was any chance she could make her slowly forming plan work. "You already got your stupid boat, what more could you want?"

Pan crossed his arms. "It is the way."

"It is the way," Slightly said, monotone.

"See?" Pan patted his back. "Slightly knows the rules. Don't have a problem with that, do you, Mother?"

She tried not to look at Slightly. She wished she could send him some kind of telepathic message that it would all be okay, that she would fix this, no matter what it took. "No." Then, with the taste of vomit in her mouth, she asked, "When?"

"Tomorrow night. Tonight, I have things to take care of." He snatched the machete hanging from Slightly's belt and tossed it to Nibs. "You're in charge."

Nibs punched the air.

Tootles scowled. "Aw, but Pan..."

"Enough. Get some rest. Tomorrow's a big day."

Pan winked at Madge before disappearing through the hatch.

Chapter Thirty

I F HOOK STILL HAD A heart, it would've been hammering like the chain of an anchor as it was reeled back to the ship. He'd dropped Madge at the island proper with a fire in her heart and a plan of action. Now, it was Hook's turn.

The Red Men camp was unusually quiet. Smaller numbers and a sober calm had turned the lively little civilization into a mausoleum. Their sacred fire was now little more than smoldering coals on which they no longer bothered to sacrifice their skin. Behind the fire pit stood a monument of stone and glass in the shape of a vague face. Its surface was covered with dozens of red handprints.

Some of the Red Men shied away from Hook as he drifted through the camp, though most had gotten used to his presence. They were a spiritual people, who believed that souls only clung to the mortal world if they were needed. Elder used to question Hook endlessly about his life before Neverland and would pretend to be shocked and appalled at the idea that he wasn't always a pirate. Hook would miss him.

He found Tiger Lily seated beside a small fire. There was a rabbit on a spit, charred, and a little girl in her lap.

The girl smiled at Hook. He smiled back.

"Her name's Violet," Tiger Lily said. "Her mother and father didn't make it."

"Charmed, Violet." Hook offered his one hand. The girl giggled at it. "She looks like you."

"What do you want, Hook?"

"It's time."

"Time for what?"

He looked pointedly at the girl. Tiger Lily sighed.

"Go see Auntie Shada," she said to Violet. "I heard she found a red-berry bush yesterday."

Violet raised an eyebrow but obeyed.

"Are you certain she's not yours?" Hook asked.

"Time for what, pirate?"

"The Darling girl is going to try to trap Pan in her world. Age him. Maybe kill him."

Tiger Lily's golden gaze flicked up. "What does that have to do with me?"

"She'll need your help."

She shook her head. "I'm not involving myself again. My people have been through too much pain because of me already. I won't be the cause of their extinction."

"But if you allow Pan's reign of terror to continue, you assure it."

"You don't know that."

"I do. And so do you."

Tiger Lily sighed. The fight with Pan had taken a lot out of her, and not just physically. It was as though he'd reached inside and snuffed out her fire.

Hook continued, "She's going to try to use his new ship as a way to lure him there. Someone needs to be on the ship to bring it back to Neverland before he has a chance to return with it."

"So you do it."

He reached for the rabbit's head. His hand passed through. "Would if I could, love."

"Have Madge do it, then."

"Tiger Lily..."

She threw a rock into the fire. "I'll consider it. That's all I can give you."

Hook nodded. "Tonight. Before dark."

And by consider it, Tiger Lily meant dismiss the idea as ridiculous. Pan was smart. He'd see through anything she and the Darling girl did. Violet returned soon after Hook left, face stained red with sweet juice.

She kissed Tiger Lily's face. "Auntie Shada says the ghost brings bad luck."

Tiger Lily smirked. "Auntie Shada thinks her fingernail clippings bring bad luck."

"Know what I think?"

"Hmm?"

"I think he's nice."

Tiger Lily stroked the girl's hair. It was long and soft and shiny black, the way Violet's mother's had been.

Maybe it was Violet's influence—the girl had a sense of stubbornness—but Tiger Lily's mind turned. If Hook was right and the Darling girl had finally gotten smart, then there might be a chance. She had a fierceness about her that didn't come from Wendy or Jane and could very well be the thing that saved them all. The question, of course, was whether Tiger Lily could be a part of it.

The sun set late, and Violet disappeared into Tiger Lily's hut, snoring before her head hit the pillow. Tiger Lily walked to Shada's and asked a favor that Shada was more than happy to give. Despite their losses, the Red Men were still a united people. They looked out for one another without complaint, without regard for their own personal comfort.

And that was why, when her father's voice in her head told her to reconsider, Tiger Lily set off for Pan's ship.

From the diary of Wendy Moira Angela Darling

It was the middle of the night when someone knocked on the door. George was already asleep. He's a predictable man—supper at seven, cuppa at eight, and in bed by nine. I don't hate it. But yes, a knock at the door in the middle of the night. Strange to anyone except me, I suppose, for I've always hoped that one day there'd be such a knock, and on the other side would be—

No. I can't even write it. Can't even think it.

It wasn't him. It was Jane, and she was fat with child.

At first I suspected Slightly. He was always the one blushing over little things like a bare calf or the way my curls fell around my shoulders. He didn't think I noticed, but I did.

"It's him," Jane said. "It's his."

I brushed her off. "Don't worry, dear. We'll take care of it."

I wasn't as old fashioned as Jane liked to think. She was too far along for us to do anything permanent about the child, but somewhere, someone would take it in. If not a proper home, then an orphanage. They're not all that bad, really. You hear stories, but you can't always believe what you hear in stories, can you?

"I don't want to take care of it," Jane said. Stupid girl.

I tried to assure her that she could not let her bastard be the reason she was shunned from polite society.

"You don't understand." She started to cry. "It's Peter's."

I struggle to put into words the torrent of emotion I felt upon hearing that accusation. Peter's child, indeed. At first, I thought she was lying. But I know my daughter, and she wasn't lying. Once the impossible was accepted, a blind rage cycloned in my belly—in my very womb where I'd cradled this woman in infancy. Loved and protected her. Provided for her. And how does she repay me?

Treachery. Villainous, hateful, spiteful, jealous little harlot. I could've strangled her in that moment. My own flesh and blood. I couldn't see for all the hatred I felt.

I wanted to leave her on the porch, to make her sleep in the rain like the bitch she was. But then George, dutiful George, awoke and came downstairs to find his only daughter—light of his life, the poor fool—standing dirty and pregnant on his step.

"Let the child in, Wendy, my goodness."

I, of course, obeyed.

The decision has been made—without me, I'll mention—that Jane will stay with us until such time as she gives birth and we can make arrangements for the child. Jane is insistent upon keeping it (George will likely fold to her whim), but I have other plans. Once that child is born, no matter what becomes of it, Jane will be sent back to Neverland somehow. I can't stand to look at her every day, knowing my beloved's hands have touched her in a way that was meant only for me.

It's for her own good, really, because if Jane were to stay here a second longer than necessary, I would probably kill her myself.

Chapter Thirty-One

SLIGHTLY HAD KNOWN IT WAS coming the way he'd come to know the inevitable sudden wind change that came with Pan's highs and lows. He'd made a mistake. Madge was just a girl. Why had he risked himself by caring about her? That'd always been Slightly's downfall. He cared. Where the other boys cast the bulk of their empathy aside once Neverland sank its claws into their minds, Slightly had gripped his with a surprising strength. It was natural to him to care. He'd been the one to make paper fingers for Michael to slide over his nubs when Pan cut off the boy's fingers. He'd been the one to hold Jane toward the end of her life. Still, a Lost Boy wasn't supposed to care about Mothers. That was Pan's job.

So even before Pan's announcement, Slightly had felt it coming. Now that the moment had arrived, though, he couldn't accept it. He left them all in the tree house and stormed outside. He needed air.

The sky had darkened, and the air held the potential for a storm. Stupidly, Slightly wondered if he could bring the rain with his own hatred. Why did Pan have control over Neverland? What made him so special?

Slightly stomped on a fallen branch, barely cracking it. That was what made Pan special. He didn't crack things; he obliterated them. He had the courage to destroy all that was in his way. Slightly would have given his left arm for that kind of strength.

But maybe he already had it. Madge did, and she was a girl. Not just any girl, but a girl nonetheless. She'd stood up to Pan in the few days she'd been in Neverland more than Slightly ever had.

He closed his eyes and, for the first time in what felt like a thousand years, pushed the Lost Boy to the back of his mind and tried to think like Edward. He'd been ready to literally keep his sister prisoner to save her from herself. Pan had gotten in the way then, just as he was getting in the way of Madge and the Darlings' salvation now. Edward had allowed it because he had been the kind of boy that, for all his good intentions, was too weak to see his task to the end. Slightly wouldn't make the same mistake.

Slightly stood, prepared to confront Pan and all the consequences that came with it, and came face to face with Pan's shadow. The thing was like a storm cloud, all rumbles, blackness, and foreboding. Slightly froze as his gaze met the black holes where the shadow's eyes ought to have been. The corners of his vision flickered in and out of focus, making his mind spin, and he would've collapsed if the shadow hadn't gripped him by the sides of his head. The shadow's hands were like a cold spider's web that wove over his skull and into his ears, caressing Slightly's mind. He struggled, but the shadow's grip was like stone. His mind swam, and he felt bits of memory and thought being plucked and discarded. His mother's middle name. The sound of his sister's laugh. His scorn for Pan eroded like rocks beneath a waterfall, and no matter how Slightly fought, eventually his courage followed suit.

Finally released, Slightly sank against the fallen branch, his lips pulled painfully downward in an expression not matching how he felt. His fingers found the crack, and as he stroked it, a splinter jabbed itself beneath his nail. He barely felt it.

That night, Madge didn't sleep.

Coming from outside the tree house, she heard the scrape and chop of gallows being erected. Slightly oversaw the base construction before joining Madge inside. His face was ashen and cold, and he barely blinked. He stood for a long time and then sat for a moment only to stand again.

Madge watched, twirling her mother's ring on her little finger. "I don't understand you at all."

Silence.

"You have just as much reason as anyone to want to help me, but now, you're giving in?"

Slightly's expression was plastic. His lips barely moved as he spoke. "It's the way."

"God, do you hear yourself? *It is the way.* Please. If Curly or Jinx had said that, you would've knocked their heads together." Madge studied his movement, his eyes, and there was something wrong about it all. It was as if the light had been turned off inside. What had Pan done?

He took a step but stopped. "I told you. I've got nothing waiting for me. And this plan of yours—making Pan grow up—is impossible. You don't know him. He won't let it happen."

"So you're taking the coward's way out. Get out now. Never mind the others out there or the ones Pan takes next."

"It's not my job—"

"You're right. It's not. But that doesn't mean it's not the right thing to do. If you want to die, don't expect me to watch it."

Her eyes burned, but she refused to let the tears fall. On her way to the hatch, she shoved his pocketknife into his hand, which was cold as ice. She had to force his fingers to close over the knife.

Outside, the air was thick with the smell of bark and moss. Tootles and Nibs argued over the length of the rope. Tootles suggested they make Slightly come outside to measure.

She'd hoped to include the boys in her plan, maybe take them back to her world with them. But Pan's influence was too strong here. As long as Pan was young, powerful, and ruling over Neverland, they'd never be able to see reason. Not even Slightly, it seemed. If her plan worked, though, there was hope.

She looked up. Pan shot through the sky, glittering like a comet. Dust fell from him, sprinkling the ground with gold and silver. A flake touched Tootles, and he hovered a second before falling on his back.

"I'm workin' here!" he called.

Pan landed in front of Madge, and the ground vibrated. Gold dust glinted in his eyelashes. She forced her fury down deep. If this was going to work, she couldn't lose it.

"Get what you need?" she asked.

"And then some." He patted a bulging satchel at his waist. "Little heavy for the trip, though. I'll need to store some in the tree house."

"I'll do it," she said, trying not to seem too eager. "Why don't you take a look at the boys' work? They could use your input."

Pan studied her face, and for a heart-shattering second, it seemed like he knew she was hiding something. He unclipped his satchel and handed it to her. Every muscle in her body unclenched.

"There's a box beneath my chair. Pour half the dust in it, and bring the rest back to me."

She nodded and, before he could change his mind, ran for the tree house.

Slightly stood exactly where she'd left him and didn't move while she dug beneath Pan's chair. The box was made of wood with a bird wing carved into the lid. She dumped the contents of the satchel inside and began to fill the bag with dirt.

"Too heavy," Slightly said, though the effort to talk sounded physically painful. His mouth contorted into a horrifying grimace, and his face reddened.

Madge stopped. "What is?"

He didn't look at her. "Dirt. It's heavier than fairy dust. He'll notice."

"What do I use then?"

A single tear dripped down his cheek. He hunched, clutching his stomach. "Under my bunk."

Madge reached out to touch his shoulder. "Are you okay?"

He recoiled from her hand. "Just look."

She found another box, this one clumsily assembled from driftwood and filled with hundreds of shells from the beach... and white, powdery sand.

"It's lighter," Slightly said. "Should work."

Glancing up at Slightly—his cheeks puffed with each breath, and his eyes glazed over—Madge frantically scooped the sand into the bag—careful to only fill it halfway—struggling to keep her heart from pounding out of her chest. Pan had to be wondering what was taking her so long.

She stuffed both boxes back in their places and grabbed her backpack with her mother's ring and grandmother's diary inside. Before she left, she kissed Slightly's cheek. "Thank you."

A ghost of a smile touched his face, only to fall away just as quickly.

Outside, she found Pan standing over Tootles as he hammered a joint.

"C'mon! Whack it like you whack a Red Man skull!"

Clutching the satchel, Madge called him over.

He reached out to take the satchel, but she held it away. "We need to talk first."

"It's going to happen, Mother. I know you... like... Slightly, but it has to be done."

She blinked to stop a tear. What she wouldn't have given for a hammer and the guts to use it. "I'm not arguing with you. But I think you're doing this wrong."

He frowned. "Excuse me?"

She charged forward before her courage ran out. "I know how this works, Pan. I figured it out. You need them here to keep from growing up. But even you can't stop it from happening altogether."

He clicked his tongue.

"They grow too, which messes with the balance. Look at what you're left with." She gestured to Tootles and Nibs. "Your ranks are next to nothing, and you plan on thinning them further."

"What are you suggesting?"

"You have your ship. Bring more boys back *tonight*. Besides..." She paused. She could see the gears turning in his head. "What is a mother without sons?"

Magic words.

Pan grinned. "You're right. I'll leave tonight."

He tried to grab the satchel again, but she snatched it away.

"One more thing."

He raised an eyebrow.

"I want to come with you."

He started to shake his head.

"Not to stay. To get a few things." She gestured to the patches of dirt and grime on her clothes. "Clothes, for example."

"I suppose…" He scratched his head. "Yes. It would be good for the boys to meet their mother right away. Reassure them."

"Exactly."

"Okay, Mother." He took the satchel. Madge held her breath as he clipped it to his belt. "We leave now." He started to open the satchel to dust her.

She grabbed his hand. "Already have some." She shook her ponytail, and gold dust glittered around her.

Pan tilted his head back, letting out a crow. Madge's stomach flipped as he yanked her off the ground and into the sky.

Slightly's cheek burned where Madge had kissed him. His whole face, his whole body, his soul blazed warm and tingly, and if he could, he would have rolled around in it forever. What was more, the kiss seemed to have breached whatever veil Pan's shadow had shrouded Slightly's mind in, and for the first time in hours, he was able to think clearly.

Pan's crows echoed through the tree house, and Slightly knew Madge's plan was working. She was smart. She'd finish it, and then Neverland would be free of Pan forever. But even as the sounds of his morning execution lingered, Slightly wondered if that would be a good thing. Who would control the days and nights? Who would make deals with the mermaids? Who would tell stories around the fire?

He flipped Edward's pocketknife around in his hand, feeling the smooth wood and fingering the inscription. It was nice being Edward—Eddy—for a while, but in his heart, he would always be Slightly. After tucking the knife into his driftwood box, he crawled through the hatch and out into the hot Neverland air. Tootles and Nibs were fighting again, and the gallows were barely half-finished.

"Hey!" Slightly called.

The boys turned, still gripping one another by the shirts.

"What do you say to a hunt?"

"Neverbirds?" asked Nibs.

"Flying squirrelies?" asked Tootles.

Slightly bounced his eyebrows. "Sabers."

The boys whooped and stomped and ran off into the forest, leaving the unfinished gallows behind.

Chapter Thirty-Two

THE SHIP GLOWED, GLIDING THROUGH the sky like a star, but Madge was too nervous to appreciate it. Pan stood at the wheel, spinning it back and forth to navigate between cloud clusters and shifting winds. He shot her the occasional glance, but none indicated he was on to her. As they crossed into her world, the sky darkened. Thunder crashed, and soon, a storm raged beneath the ship. Floorboards creaked as the ship rocked with the motion of the storm. Madge grabbed onto the side to keep upright, stifling a scream in her chest.

"How much longer?"

"Soon." He spun the wheel to the left. "In a hurry to get to your grandmother's house?"

"In a hurry to get back to Neverland," she said quickly.

He smiled.

At least she was playing the part well enough. But could she keep it up?

Lightning flashed, lighting up the street below. Her grandmother's house appeared through a break in the clouds, and Madge's knees nearly buckled from relief. Almost there. Then Madge noticed Uncle Michael's station wagon in the driveway and hoped Pan didn't see it.

"Pull alongside my window," she said. It'd bring them to the other side of the house and away from the car.

He nodded, spinning the wheel. The bow dipped, and soon she was close enough to touch the house's siding. The boat came in too quickly and nudged the roof.

"Oops." Pan chuckled.

"I'll be quick."

He grabbed her by the waist, encircling her. His breath was hot and stale on her face. He grinned, and his hand slid down the side of her body. Something dropped into her pocket.

"A kiss," he said.

Revulsion rocked her body.

"If you're longer than five minutes," he warned, "I'm coming in after you."

She was counting on it, and pried herself from his grasp.

"I would expect nothing less." She flashed a smile before climbing over the side and onto her windowsill, where the bars had been ripped away, leaving holes in the siding.

Thunder woke him hours ago, but Michael hadn't been able to drag himself out of bed. He was too old, too tired, too sick in the head to think anything but terrible thoughts. He considered ending it all somehow, but he was too weak to pull the trigger of George's shotgun, tucked safely away in the closet. He could down the bottle of tranquilizers he'd swiped from Wendy's room, but knowing his luck, they wouldn't be enough to kill him.

Why couldn't he have someone like himself around to save him the way he'd saved John? Thinking about his brother made Michael's stomach and head ache, but like with most things, once he started, he couldn't stop.

They'd all come back from Neverland a little shook up, Michael more than John, but less than Wendy. Eventually, they'd dealt with it in their own ways. Michael took up drinking, Wendy had her husband and daughter—God rest her soul—and John had his family. Those two kiddos had been gorgeous from the get-go, and once they were born, Michael felt that all the badness of the past could maybe fall away that little bit more.

He had been wrong. Michael was fucking tired of being wrong. Pan came for the children because why would he do anything else? Michael imagined Abigail and Nathan went willingly because to imagine anything else was too much for him to take. Once John found out, he'd vowed to return to Neverland to get them back. Wendy encouraged him, though she'd probably had her own motivations.

Michael begged him to leave well enough alone. Maybe the little ones would fare better than he and his siblings had. Abigail wasn't delicate the way Wendy had been, and Nathan was a scrapper. But John wouldn't see reason. None of them would. They would bring Pan back into their lives, and who knew what kind of hell that would rain down?

In a rare moment of sober clarity, Michael had decided something needed to be done. He hadn't enjoyed taking John's life. For all his faults, John was still Michael's brother. But Michael wouldn't risk bringing Pan back into their lives. He'd come too far, drowned so much memory in booze to destroy it.

Michael hadn't regretted it, not then, and not until the moment Madge was taken. Now he realized no matter what he did, Pan would be there, waiting.

Maybe he could do it. Maybe if he closed his eyes and swallowed the gun barrel...

He reached over to the nightstand to turn on the lamp. A loud thump from the other room made him pause. Cursing his bad ears, Michael strained to hear anything else. There was a voice. Two voices. The one—a girl—he recognized right away, and his heart soared. But then the other registered, a voice he hadn't heard in a long, long time.

Madge was back, but she'd brought Peter Pan with her.

Madge slid her other foot to the windowsill. She kicked the window open and shoved off the side of the ship, giving her body enough momentum to fall into the room. She hit the ground hard. Pain shot through her shoulder.

She stood, rubbing her arm, and surveyed the room. Aside from a few snatches of police tape across the doorway, it was exactly as she'd left it. Madge realized that this was where her plan stopped. She'd got Pan to her world. That was supposed to be the hard part. How was she supposed to keep him here?

Her first instinct was to find rope or something to tie him up with, and that was assuming she could get him still enough to tie up in the first place. The only place she could think of to find it was in the garage. She had five minutes, and a flick of the light switch told her the power was out. She was going to have to find it blind.

With one final glance toward the window—he was still on the ship—Madge groped her way to the hall. Carefully, she pulled the door mostly closed behind her. A ball of light bounced on the wall, and she followed the beam to Grandma Wendy's room. The door was cracked open, and a single bloodshot eye stared at her from the space.

"Madge?" Uncle Michael whispered.

She put a finger to her lips. "He's here," she mouthed.

The door opened an inch further, and Uncle Michael's shaky hand emerged. "Come in here. We'll hide."

She shook her head. "Do you know if Grandma keeps any rope around here? Or handcuffs?"

His spidery eyebrows scrunched together. "Please. We need to hide." He put the nubs of his two missing digits to his lips.

It dawned on Madge that her mother and grandmother weren't the only Darlings to go to Neverland. Was there any part of her life that Pan hadn't touched? Uncle Michael wasn't going to be any help, and she'd waste time trying to convince him to. He'd probably collapse at the sight of Pan—forget grabbing him.

"Okay," she said. "You go inside. Hide. I'm gonna grab a knife."

He considered this then nodded. "Be careful."

Coward, she thought, but offered a small smile. "You too."

The door closed with barely a sound, and Madge ran downstairs. The lights still weren't working, but there was just enough glow from the battery-operated emergency light outside to see by. Again, her knowledge of the house thanks to her middle-of-the-night escapes would be her saving grace. The mess in the kitchen smelled like death, and she wondered how long she'd been gone. Days? A week? Was Grandma Wendy still in the hospital? A chilling thought occurred to Madge: did she even care?

In the kitchen, Madge grabbed a steak knife but continued searching drawers. She set duct tape on the counter beside a big frying pan that looked like it'd take out a wrestler if swung properly. The kitchen door led to the garage, where an emergency light flickered on when she entered, carrying her kitchen finds. She pulled drawers out of the dusty toolbox—a rare remnant of Grandpa George—and scattered tools over the ground. If Pan could hear her, she had less time than she'd thought. Finally, tucked in the back of the biggest drawer, she found a bungee cord with thick metal hooks on both ends.

"Check. Now for the—"

"Madge?" Pan's voice called from somewhere in the house. "We don't have time for this. Let's go!"

Madge imagined Uncle Michael cowering behind the bed. She hooked one end of the bungee cord to the worktable and hoped it'd hold.

"Down here!" she called, holding the kitchen knife behind her back.

She heard his cautious footsteps—*good*, she thought, *he isn't flying*—descend the stairs and wander through the kitchen.

"Where?"

"Here." She positioned herself close to the toolbox, noting with relief that it had wheels.

The door opened wider, and Pan stood in the doorway. "You know I love a game as much as the next boy, but we don't have time for this."

Madge pushed the toolbox with all of her weight toward him. Pan was too slow to avoid it, and the thing crashed into his hip. He fell backward, clutching his side.

"Madge!" Uncle Michael called.

There was no time to answer. She scrambled toward Pan before he could get up and plunged the knife into his thigh. He screamed and tangled his fist in her hair. Pain rocketed through her skull as he yanked, driving his good knee into her cheek. Blinking back tears, she pulled the knife out and stabbed again, this time in his arm. Warm blood smeared down her face, but he let go. She threw the knife to the other side of the garage, out of his reach, and hooked her arms beneath his. Grunting with the effort, she dragged a flailing Pan toward the table. He reached for the sword at his hip, but his wriggling had loosened his belt, and the sword fell out.

Finally at the table, Madge stood and kicked the side of his face, relishing the feel of his bones crunching. He was dazed but didn't pass out. Cursing, she wrapped the bungee around him, arms pinned to his waist, over and over until there was almost no give, and then she hooked the other side to the table.

Blood pulsed from his wounds, and he blinked rapidly. "I should've known."

Madge picked up his sword and pointed it at his throat. "Yeah, you should've."

"Madge?" Uncle Michael appeared, shivering and hunched, at the door. He held a shotgun.

It took forever for Madge to catch her breath. Her body reacted on autopilot while her mind raced. "Uncle Michael, go get your car keys."

Pan's eyes fluttered open. Alert. "Michael. Long time no see, Shorty."

Uncle Michael flinched.

"Look at me," Madge said to Uncle Michael. She could not let him ruin this.

His gaze flicked to her then back to Pan.

"Nice-looking gun you got here," Pan said. "Planning to use it?"

Uncle Michael nodded.

"Good, good. See, you probably been around decades longer than you should've been, right? I mean, look at you. You're a walking corpse, Short Stuff."

Madge kicked Pan's leg wound. "Shut up!"

He didn't flinch. "Worthless then and worthless now. Couldn't even keep your granddaughter from the likes of me."

Uncle Michael howled. His arms were long and allowed him to more or less point the barrel of the gun at his own face.

"That's right, Michael. End it. End all the pain right now."

With a cry in her throat, Madge tore off a long strip of duct tape and slapped it across Pan's mouth. Then she wrapped most of the roll around his head, covering his mouth and eyes.

It wasn't until she finished that Uncle Michael seemed to recover. He let the gun slip to the ground, eyes agog and mouth agape.

Too close, Madge thought, eyeing the gun.

"Your car," she said slowly. "Get the keys."

Uncle Michael stumbled back through the house.

Madge looked down at Pan, sword back in her hand, and she thought of how easy it would be to cut his head off. *End it all, just like he said.*

But she shook off the idea—as difficult as it was—and convinced herself that it would be too easy a punishment for Pan. The boy who never grew up needed to feel the anguish of leaving boyhood forever. She'd start by bringing him to the police station and turning him in as her abductor. He'd get put away. No chance of returning to Neverland.

His face turned toward her as though looking at her through all the tape, his cheeks plumped as though pulled up in a grin.

He looked *proud*.

Chapter Thirty-Three

Iт тоок forever for Grandma to open her eyes. While they waited, Madge listened to the detective's questions without answering them. She told him that Peter Pan snatched her off the side of the road and kept her trapped somewhere until she tricked him into bringing her home.

"How did you do that?" the detective asked.

She shrugged. "Luck." It wasn't a complete lie. She couldn't shake the feeling that Pan had somehow allowed her to catch him. He'd put up a fight, but she had the sense that he'd held back. He wanted her to beat him, maybe even kill him. *But why? What would that prove?*

After a while, the doctor pulled the detective aside and told him Madge was probably still worried her abductor would come back for her and would be more likely to answer his questions in the morning after she'd had time to adjust.

Grandma's heart monitor beeped encouragingly. The doctor said not to wake her—that a sudden jolt would compromise her stability. Four days post-surgery, they still weren't confident in her condition. Four days. It'd felt like forever.

Madge had her backpack with her and withdrew Grandma Wendy's book. Most of the pages were filled with her grandmother's long, elegant script. A nurse came in to check Grandma's IV, and Madge asked her for something to drink.

Hot cocoa steamed on the table beside her as Madge settled into the chair and read.

A rustling of sheets. Soft groans. A gasp. "Margaret?"

Madge wished she couldn't believe the things she'd read. Sadly, she believed every word. How could she not? The diary was Grandma Wendy's confession. The years Madge had spent in that woman's shadow, the glares and reproachful looks... They all made sense now. Even the way Pan had looked at her during those last moments. Pride. Like a father... The thought was like poison. She wanted to cry or scream, but nothing came out. It all built in her chest until it burned. She didn't look up. She couldn't. Instead, she read aloud, "*Because if Jane were to stay here a second longer than necessary, I would probably kill her myself.*"

She forced herself to meet her grandmother's gaze. A cacophony of emotions played in the old woman's wrinkles. The only one Madge didn't see was remorse.

"That's what you said when she came to you for help. When Pan—or should I say Dad?—left her to fend for herself with me growing inside. He killed her. Did you know that? And it's your fault."

Grandma Wendy shook her head. The oxygen line tinged against the bed frame.

"He's here, you know."

At this, Grandma Wendy's mouth slackened. Her eyes moistened, crinkling at the corners.

"Not at the hospital, obviously. But here. In this world. He's going to grow up."

"How..."

Madge stood and threw the book. It hit the bedside tray and knocked over a cup of water, which splattered on the floor. "By doing what you should have done the minute he brought you back. You saw the things he did to the boys. You *helped* him."

"I loved him."

Disgusting. "He's a monster."

"Even beasts can feel love."

"He can't. All he can feel is anger." She approached the bed, fists clenched. She saw red. "I suppose he and I are alike that way because right now, all I want to do is—"

All outside thoughts were gone. Madge yanked the IV line from Grandma Wendy's vein. Blood spurted, barely missing her face. The heart monitor beeped faster as Grandma Wendy's heart rate climbed. Madge took a few stiff steps back. She wanted to scream. To throw things.

Grandma Wendy's face contorted into something painful to watch. The heart monitor flatlined, and voices shouted outside the door.

Madge ran.

Slightly and the boys were gathered around a small fire when Tiger Lily approached. The boys scowled, and Tootles reached for his knife, but Slightly stopped him.

"Pan's gone?" Slightly asked her, his heart in his throat.

Tiger Lily nodded. "The ship has been returned to the lagoon."

Every muscle, every bone in his body experienced exquisite relief. It was over. Pan was gone, he would live, and nothing would ever be the same again. He frowned. "And Madge?"

"I don't know."

What if Pan had done something to her? What if Wendy... No, she was probably old by now and unlikely to hurt Madge. Probably.

Slightly said, "Would you be able to take me to her?"

Tiger Lily studied him for what felt like hours. "You do not wish to bring Pan back, do you?"

"No." The weight of the word fell like a boulder. "Never. I just want... to see her."

She nodded once. "You'll have to consult with the pirate. The ship is his now. If he grants you the ship, once you return, you will owe me a favor."

His heart soared. "Anything."

"When you return, no matter what the pirate says, burn it."

Slightly agreed.

Slightly came for her in the middle of the night. The ship hovered beside her bedroom window, aglow with flecks of fairy dust. By morning, the cops would figure out where she'd gone and try to take her back to the hospital, or worse, put her in care until Wendy was discharged. Madge didn't plan to stick around that long. It was a stroke of luck that Slightly appeared when he did. Otherwise, she might have done something stupid, like hitchhike.

"I wanted to check on you," he said after she released him from a bone-crushing hug. "Make sure everything… that Pan's…"

"He's stuck here for good," Madge said. "If they don't keep him in jail forever for kidnapping, they'll at least keep tabs on him. It'll be next to impossible for him to get back."

They were quiet for a long time. Madge caught his eye and smiled. He turned away, face red.

"The, uh, the boys say hello."

"Hello back."

He nodded. "Right. I'll tell 'em."

"Eddy?"

"It's still Slightly."

She grinned. "Okay. Slightly?"

"Yeah?"

"I'll tell them myself."

He smiled, but it quickly dipped into a frown. "But you're—"

"I forgive you for not telling me about Pan and my grandmother. I probably wouldn't have listened anyway." He opened his mouth, but she covered it. "I'm coming with you."

Slightly's eyes lit, and the corners of his mouth curled into a shy smile. He was handsome, but Madge wouldn't tell him she thought so. Not yet, anyway. He offered her his hand. "Your ship awaits, m'lady."

Madge watched the house fall away for the second time as the ship climbed higher into the black-blue expanse toward the second star that would lead them to a new Neverland. It occurred to her that it might not be the same, might not even exist without Pan. But in her heart, Madge believed it could. She believed that Neverland would bloom and brighten, and she laughed with the possibility of it all.

"Learn any new stories while you were away?" Slightly asked.

"Just the one, but it hasn't finished yet."

"Can I hear it?"

Madge closed her eyes, welcoming the warmth of the star on her skin. "All girls grow up... except one."

Hook was cautiously optimistic, which was unusual, even for him. The tone in Neverland was one of quiet, anxious anticipation. The waters were calm and the birds hidden in their nests. In the distance, smoke rose from the new home of the Red Man camp, perched on a cliff overlooking Skull Rock. Tiger Lily brought back the ship, as promised. He made a mental note to thank her personally.

Pan had been gone longer than ever, and while the moon and the sun shuddered as they struggled to find their natural order, the existence of the world held steady. The wind picked up. There would be heavy storms this afternoon, but they would pass. Neverland would continue.

Hook knew he shouldn't have given the ship over to the boy. Even if he was the most civilized of that disgusting horde, Slightly was still a Lost Boy, and Lost Boys weren't meant to be trusted. With Smee at his side, he scanned the skies, waiting for that pop in air pressure—felt only by ghosts and mermaids—that signaled their return.

When it finally came, Hook strained to see the figures at the helm. One was Slightly. The other was the Darling girl.

"Somethin' the matter, Cap'n?" Smee asked.

"Cast your eyes skyward. Tell me what you see."

"Pan's boat, Cap'n."

"And?"

Smee squinted. "Looks like the young brute has returned with little Miss Madge." He gasped. "You don't think he kidnapped her, do you? Of all the barnacle-sniffing—"

"She wasn't kidnapped, Smee."

"Oh. Well, that's good then, isn't it?"

Hook sighed. He'd give his very soul to regain his physical form just long enough to wallop his idiot first mate. "It's happening again, Smee. Don't you feel it?"

Smee shivered. "But... she's a girl. Girls are different."

Hook smirked. Not as different as they would have you believe. Those of the female persuasion, in Hook's *advanced* experience, had the capacity and imagination for deeds more devious than even he—Captain James Hook—could conjure.

"Perhaps you're right, Smee. Still."

The ship glided over the densest part of the forest, shedding that wretched gold dust that was impossible to get out of silk, before dipping behind the trees and out of sight. Hook couldn't help noticing the sky brighten—and the breeze warm—at her presence.

"We'll keep an eye on her. Won't we, Smee?"

Smee saluted. "Aye, Cap'n."

Epilogue

PETER FELL INTO MARRYING MARITZA the way he falls into most things: drunk and on a bet. What started out as playful, Jose Cuervo-fueled banter—I bet you won't tell me you love me; I bet you won't kiss me here; I bet you won't marry me—turned into a giggly "I do," a plastic ring, and a skull-smashing hangover.

His buddy said to get an annulment—he knew a guy who could push the paperwork through quick—but Peter didn't really mind the marriage. Maritza's ass was like two cantaloupes hugging each other, and she could cook franks n' mac like no one he'd ever met. She was a catch, and he'd caught her. Now he just had a piece of paper to prove it.

Ten years later, her ass is still like two cantaloupes, except now they've gone soft and flat around the bottom. Her stomach is striped with the comings and goings of their three kids. Her breasts point to the ground except when she's on her back, and then they point to either side. Peter doesn't mind, not really. He likes the way she smells of *Mommy*—sour/sweet milk and sweat and a long-dead ghost of perfume. It's the kids that drive him insane.

Today is no different.

After spending years as a piss-ant delivery driver, Peter finally scored a union job at the cheese plant. It's mind-numbing work, but it's *protected* mind-numbing work. With *benefits*. He can finally get that impacted molar taken out, once the insurance company sends him his card.

He works swing shifts, which means he's sleeping—or trying to—

when the kids are at their energy peak. With Maritza working part-time as a receptionist, the nine-year-old, Marie, gets left in charge.

"Goddammit, Pablo!" Her voice punches through the thin wall dividing Peter's room from the living room. She's got a mouth like her mother, but a man's got to pick his battles. "Mom's gonna kill you!"

Pablo's five and decided while still in diapers that his purpose in life would be to make the lives of his parents a living hell. Rather than investigate what the little shit's gotten into, Peter piles pillows around his head, cursing himself for not picking up a bottle of liquid sleep on his way home.

He finally drifts off and dreams the same dream he's had every day for as long as he can remember—which isn't long at all. Ask him anything about before getting stuck at St. Mary's, and he'll shrug. Selective amnesia, the doctors had called it. Peter had wondered about it for a while, but then life happened, and he didn't care to worry about a blank past. He could be whoever he wanted to be, and that suited him just fine.

The dream always starts with him staring up at a star-filled sky. They swirl and bleed into the blue-black of the sky like the painting by that guy who went crazy and chopped off his ear. Then it rains red. Big, fat drops sting against his face and neck before turning gold and soft. His stomach lurches, and—this is his favorite part—he lifts up from the ground like a balloon and flies toward one star. Always the same one. It's warm and inviting, and he reaches out to touch it because he knows deep in his belly that something wonderful will happen if he does. So close and his eyes water from the brightness and—

"Peter."

So close, he can almost feel—

"Peter!"

He gurgles. The room comes into focus. Maritza hovers over him. Her long black hair is tied at the top of her head, and her shirt is open with the baby latched to a nipple. She used to let Peter taste it. Now she rolls her eyes and calls him a pervert.

"You're gonna be late, stupid."

Stupid. That's the other thing she calls him. Asshole. Prick. A thousand others. He's only ever called her darling—at first because it fit and now because it annoys her.

"Your daughter was supposed to wake me up." He zombies to a sitting position, spine cracking.

"So she's my daughter now, eh? Not even going to claim your own children?"

He shakes his head. He doesn't have time for a fight. "I gotta go."

"Yeah, you go." The baby starts to cry, and Maritza stuffs the nipple back in. "Make sure you bring back the man I married, okay?"

Peter snorts. As if he's the one who's changed. "Yeah, darling. Okay. I'll do that."

The car doesn't start on the first try. He slams a fist into the steering wheel, jiggles the gas pedal, then tries again. A plume of black smoke erupts from the exhaust, but it starts. As he pulls out of the driveway, which dips at the end, the contents of the trunk slam against the back seat.

Once he's a little ways down the road, Peter parks on a dark street and opens the trunk. The girl's face is smashed in—he'd gotten a little carried away with the hammer—but it's mostly obscured by blond hair that's glued to her chin and forehead with blood. Part of him is disappointed Maritza didn't find her. He'd left the girl there—in their shared car—on purpose. It's killing him to keep it a secret. For a while, he thought he'd be able to share it with Maritza. She's vicious in her own way. But after the third kid, she turned her viciousness on him. He wants to scare her, to make sure she knows he's the powerful one.

On the other hand, if she finds out, he'll have to stop. He's not sure he wants to stop.

He stops at the liquor store and buys a bottle of Jose, a third of which is consumed in the parking lot—another third on the drive toward the plant. It's a great job, he keeps telling himself. No one bothers him. Temps fly in and out of the place—like the one in his trunk—and no one pays enough attention to care. But as the tequila replaces his blood, the dream—that fucking dream—drifts into his consciousness. It doesn't make sense. Nothing. He's got—no, he had something, something good and important, but that something's gone now. Doesn't even know what it is.

He's swerving over the road. He looks up, and the stars are twisting just like his dream. It's real, he thinks. This is the nightmare, and that's real.

There's a bridge ahead. Peter pulls over, leaving the bottle and the girl behind, and walks toward it.

Michael follows Peter Pan's car at a reasonable distance. He's been at this awhile and gotten pretty good at not getting caught.

Wendy died in the hospital the night Madge came back. Heart attack, the doctors said, but her heart was too weak to withstand another blow. Madge ran away. Michael knows where she went but told the police he was clueless. After all the things he hasn't done to protect her, it was the one thing he could offer her. The police stopped asking after a while. Crazy old man, they called him. Not a stretch to believe the *old man* is losing his mind a bit.

And Christ, but he is getting old. Tried to take his license last year if he didn't master some rigged course meant to weed out good, taxpaying people like himself. Luckily, he passed. Barely.

His glasses fog up, and he cranks the heater to clear them. Pan almost never goes this way on his own. He's supposed to be going to work. A shitty factory job, but he stays out of trouble. Mostly. Lots of missing girls around here lately. Sometimes, Michael wonders if Pan remembers. If he does, they're all in for some trouble.

Around the bend, Pan is stopped at the end of a bridge. He climbs out and makes a beeline for the railing. Michael eases onto a shoulder, out of the way, but close enough that he can still see. If Pan knows Michael's there, he obviously doesn't care. Pan climbs up onto the railing and stares out over the water.

It's an hour before the police show up. One of them tries to convince Michael to go home, but he plays the lost-old-man bit well. He nods his head a little then squints. Says he needs to find his dog, Nana. Eventually, the cop agrees to let him hang out, but warns him not to go near the bridge until they've cleared it.

"No problem," Michael says. "Thank you."

Pan still stands on the railing, wobbling a little, but doesn't look like he's planning on jumping yet. The cops stand around, hands on hips, waiting for someone official to show up.

Soon, a man one of the cops calls "the negotiator" strolls onto the bridge. He's tall, clean-shaven, cocky—the kind of guy who takes the business of saving lives as seriously as his haircut. Pan will eat him for dinner.

Michael is unable to tear his eyes from Pan. A small voice in his mind whispers, *Jump!* He dares to hope that this will finally be the end, that he'll finally be able to move on.

The negotiator talks through a megaphone, but it's as if Pan can't hear him. He's leaning forward, kept on the bridge by an unstable grip of three fingers.

"This isn't the way," the negotiator says. "We can help you."

Pan turns, and his icy gaze falls on Michael, freezing him to his very soul. Pan releases his grip, falling forward with arms spread wide.

Michael holds his breath.

There's no splash.

Acknowledgements

Without J.M. Barrie's original novel, this story wouldn't exist. I am extraordinarily grateful for the world he created in Neverland and the characters who became my instant friends and constant companions throughout my childhood. I want to thank my editor, Karen Allen, who couldn't have been more perfect to sift through this tale and share the joy in the little details that, hopefully, give *All Darling Children* the sparkle it deserves. Thank you, Renee Miller, beta-reader, friend, and taker of middle-of-the-night messages that begin, "Yeah, but WHAT IF..." Also huge thanks to readers Hanna Elizabeth and Rob Hart for your spot-on suggestions.

Finally, I give enormous gratitude to my wife, Crystal, for her constant encouragement and not always groaning when I want to watch *Peter Pan* again.

About the Author

Katrina Monroe is a novelist, mom, and snark-slinger extraordinaire.

Her worst habits include: eating pretty much anything with her fingers, yelling at inappropriate times, and being unable to focus on important things like dinner and putting on pants.

She collects quotes like most people collect, well, other things. Her favorite is, "If you have any young friends who aspire to become writers, the second greatest favor you can do them is to present them with copies of *The Elements of Style*. The first greatest, of course, is to shoot them now, while they're happy." – Dorothy Parker

Readers can revel in her sarcasm at authorkatrinamonroe.wordpress.com or follow her on Twitter: @authorkatm.

Made in the USA
Lexington, KY
20 September 2017